KING PENGUIN

GENTLEMEN OF
THE WEST

Agnes Owens was born on Empire Day in 1926, the year when the Depression was at its worst. Although as a child she was not aware of any hardship, her political outlook was coloured by the general poverty and misery she recalls on looking back. Her only ambition at school was to leave and she has worked in a factory, as a shorthand typist and as a school cleaner among other things. She has been married twice and has seven children.

She says that although she always had a notion of creating something artistic, she came to writing by accident and would have preferred to have been a painter. She joined a writers' class and wrote a series of stories which turned out to be *Gentlemen of the West*. Her previous short stories were originally published in Arts Council magazines and are now collected in a volume called *Lean Tales* which also includes work by Alasdair Gray and Jim Kelman.

Agnes Owens received an Autumn Book Award from the Scottish Arts Council for *Gentlemen of the West* and is now working on a continuation volume, *Birds in the Wilderness*.

AGNES OWENS

———

GENTLEMEN OF THE WEST

A KING PENGUIN
PUBLISHED BY PENGUIN BOOKS

Oh wert thou in the cauld blast.
—Robert Burns

Penguin Books Ltd, Harmondsworth, Middlesex, England
Viking Penguin Inc., 40 West 23rd Street, New York, New York 10010, U.S.A.
Penguin Books Australia Ltd, Ringwood, Victoria, Australia
Penguin Books Canada Limited, 2801 John Street, Markham, Ontario, Canada L3R 1B4
Penguin Books (N.Z.) Ltd, 182–190 Wairau Road, Auckland 10, New Zealand

First published by Polygon Books 1984
Published in Penguin Books 1986

Made and printed in Great Britain by
Richard Clay (The Chaucer Press) Ltd,
Bungay, Suffolk
Typeset in Times

Contents

1   McDONALD'S DUG

2   McDONALD'S MASS

3   GRIEVOUS BODILY HARM

4   TOLWORTH McGEE

5   THE AULD WIFE'S FANCY MAN

6   UP COUNTRY

7   THE GROUP

8   PAID AFF

9   McCLUSKIE'S OOT

10   CHRISTMAS DAY IN THE PAXTON

11   THE AFTERMATH

12   THE GHOST SEEKER

13   GOODBYE EVERYBODY

Postscript by Alasdair Gray to Agnes Owen's
Gentlemen of the West

1

McDonald's dog was not the type of animal that people took kindly to, or patted on the head with affection. It was more likely to receive the odd kick, along with the words "gerr oot", which it accepted for the most part with indifference. If the kick was too well aimed it bared its teeth in a chilling manner which prevented further kicks. Large, grey and gaunt it roamed the streets, foraged the dustbins and hung around the local co-operative to the disgust of customers coming and going. The manager, who received continual complaints about it, as if it was his responsibility, would throw pails of water over it to pacify plaintive statements such as, "Ye'd better dae somethin' aboot that dug. It's a bloody disgrace the way it hings aboot this shop." Though he had no heart for this action, as more often than not he missed the dog, which had the sensuary perception of a medium and could move like a streak of lightning, causing innocent housewives to be soaked instead. Even so, McDonald's dog was a valuable asset to its owner. With its height and leanness, plus a sharp, evil face, it

7

might have been a greyhound on the loose, but in fact its character was determined from a lurcher ancestor, an animal talented in the art of poaching. I had an interest in McDonald's dog due to the following incident.

One particularly dreich evening I was waiting at the bus stop, soaked to the skin. My bones ached from damp clothing. All day I had been sitting in the hut at the building site waiting for the rain to stop in order to get on with the vocation of laying the brick, but it never halted. We played cards, ate soggy pieces and headed with curses for the toilet. On that site it was wherever you happened to find a convenient spot.

So I was thankful when Willie Morrison drew up with his honky-tonk motor like something out of Wacky Races.

"Jump in Mac," he said.

I did so with alacrity, hoping the door would not fall on my feet. It was that type of motor.

"Thanks Wullie."

We proceeded in silence since Willie had a job to see where he was going. The windscreen wipers did not work too well. I was on the point of falling asleep when suddenly we hit a large object.

"Watch where yer gaun," I said, very much aggrieved that my head had banged against the window. A spray of liquid spurted over our vision. For a sickening minute I thought it was blood, then I realised it was water from the radiator.

"My God, that's done it," croaked Willie. Panicking I opened the door regardless of the danger to my feet. I was just in time to see the shadow of an animal limp towards the hedge.

"Ye've hit an animal o' some kind," I said.

"Whit wis it — a coo?"

"Don't be daft. This motor wid have nae chance against a coo. I think it wis a dug."

"Och a dug. It's nae right bein' on the road."

He started up the engine and with a great amount of spluttering the car roared off at thirty miles an hour. I felt a bit gloomy at the thought of a dog maybe bleeding to death in the sodden hedgerow, but Willie was only concerned for his car.

"This motor's likely jiggered noo."

I couldn't be bothered to point out that it was jiggered before. I was only wishing I had taken the bus. We reached our destination without saying much. Hunger had overcome my thoughts on the dog. I hoped my mother had something tasty for the dinner, which would be unlikely.

Some days later I happened to be in McDonald's company. McDonald was like his dog, very difficult at times. But in the convivial atmosphere of the Paxton Arms we were often thrown together, and under the levelling influence of alcohol we would view each other with friendly eyes. Though you had to take your chances with him. On occasions his eyes would be more baleful than friendly. Then, if your senses were not completely gone, you discreetly moved away. McDonald labelled himself a ploughman. To prove it he lived in a ramshackle cottage close to a farm. Though the word cottage was an exaggeration. It was more like an old bothy. Some folk said he was a squatter, and some folk said he was a tinker, but never to his face. On this occasion I was not too sure about his mood. He appeared sober, but depressed.

"How's things?" I asked, testing him out to see if I

should edge nearer to him.

"Could be better."

"How's that then?" I asked.

"It's that dug o' mine."

"Yer dug?"

"Aye. Some bastard run him ower."

"That's terrible Paddy." My brain was alert to danger.

"As ye know yersel," continued McDonald, unobservant of the shifty look in my eyes, "ma dug is no' ordinary dug. It's a good hard-working dug. In fact," his chest heaved with emotion, "ye could say that dug has kept me body and soul when I hudny a penny left."

I nodded sympathetically. McDonald's dole money was often augmented by rabbits, hares and pheasants that he sold at half the butcher's price.

"An' d'ye know," he stabbed my chest with a grimy finger, "I've hud tae fork oot ten pounds for a vet. Think o' that man — ten pounds!"

I didn't believe him about the ten pounds, but I was relieved the dog wasn't dead.

"Where's the dug noo?" I asked.

"The poor beast's restin' in the hoose."

I remembered his house. On one or two occasions I had partaken of his hospitality. A bottle of wine had been the passport. He kept live rabbits in the oven — lucky for them it was in disuse — pigeons in a cage in the bedroom, and a scabby cat always asleep at the end of a lumpy sofa, with the dog at the other end. I don't know if this menagerie lived in harmony, but they had survived so far. I thought at this stage I had better buy him a drink to take the edge off his bitterness before I shifted my custom. It was obvious his mood would not improve with all this on his mind. McDonald swallowed the beer appreciatively but he was reluctant to change the subject.

"An' I'm tellin' ye, if I get ma haunds on the rat that done it I'll hing him."

"It's a right rotten thing tae happen." To get out of it all I added, "I wish I could stay an' keep ye company, but I huv tae gie Jimmy Wilson a haun' wi' his fence, so see ye later."

Swiftly I headed for the Trap Inn hoping I would see Willie Morrison to break the bad news to him. However, it was a couple of days before I met Willie again. He was waiting at the bus stop motorless, and with the jaundiced look of a man who has come down in the world. He grunted an acknowledgement.

"Huv ye no' got yer motor?" I asked.

"Naw."

He shuffled about, then explained. "Mind that night we hit that dug?"

I nodded.

"Well, the motor has been aff the road ever since. And dae ye know whit it'll cost me tae get it fixed?"

"Naw," I said, although I was not all that much agog.

"Twenty nicker."

He stared at me for sympathy. Dutifully I rolled my eyes around.

"That's some lolly."

"Anyway I've pit it in the haunds of ma lawyer." His eyes were hard and vengeful.

Before any more was said the bus rumbled up. Justice was forgotten. We kicked, jostled and punched to get on, and I was first. Before Willie managed to put his foot on the platform I turned to him saying, "I heard it wis McDonald's dug ye run ower."

In his agitation he sagged and was shoved to the back of the queue.

"That's enough," shouted the hard-faced conductress. The bus drove off leaving Willie stranded.

"I hear that somebody battered Johnny Morrison last night," said my mother conversationally as she dished out the usual indigestible hash that passed for a meal by her standards.

"Whit's this then?" I asked, ignoring the information.

"Whit dae ye mean 'whit's this'? It's yer dinner."

"I don't want it."

"D'ye know whit I've paid for it?"

"Naw, an' I don't want tae."

"You really sicken me. Too much money an' too many Chinese takeaways, that's your trouble."

"Shut up, an' gies a piece o' toast."

"Oh well, if that's all ye want then," she said, mollified.

She was very good at toast.

Then her opening remark dawned on me. "Whit wis that ye said aboot Johnny Morrison?"

She poured out the tea, which flowed from the spout like treacle. "Jist as I said. He opened the door aboot eleven at night an' somebody battered him."

"Whit for?" I asked. I would have seen the connection if it had been Willie.

"How should I know. He got the polis in but he didny recognise the man. He had a pair o' tights ower his heid."

"Tights," I echoed. "Do ye no' mean nylons?"

Stranger and stranger I thought. I could hardly see Paddy McDonald wearing either tights or nylons, just to give somebody a doing. Anyway, two odd socks were his usual concession to style. And why batter Willie's brother? Not unless he was out to get the whole family.

I was soon put out of my bewilderment. On Saturday night I saw Paddy McDonald in the Paxton, swaying like a reed in the wind. His expression was one of benignity for all mankind, but like a bloodhound or his lurcher he spied me straightaway.

"There ye are son. Here whiddy ye want tae drink?"

Straightaway I said, "A hauf an' a hauf pint." I was in a reckless mood and heedless of hazards. It was a Saturday, and I was out to enjoy myself. I was going to get bevvied.

He took a roll of notes from his pocket and waved one of them in the direction of the barman like a flag of victory.

"You seem to be loaded," I said.

"Aye."

"Did somebody kick the bucket and leave you a fortune?"

"It's no' a' that much," he replied modestly. "Only twenty pounds."

"How dae ye manage tae have that on a Saturday?"

McDonald's money was usually long gone by that time. He got his dole money on a Friday.

He was lost in a reverie of happy fulfilment. Before he could make any disclosures Johnny Morrison entered. Both his eyes were a horrible shade of yellowish green and there was a bit of sticking plaster above one of them. McDonald regarded him with concern. "That's a terrible face ye have on ye Johnny."

13

"D'ye think I don't know. Ye don't have tae tell me!" replied Johnny with emotion.

"Have a drink John," said McDonald. "Wi' a face like that ye deserve one."

He waved another pound at the barman.

After doing his duty by Johnny he turned to me and put an arm round my shoulder.

"I wis really sorry aboot Johnny," he whispered.

"Wis it you that done it then?"

"Dear God naw, though I know how it happened." Dreamily he paused.

"How?" Now I was interested and hoped he would not sag to the floor before he could tell me. He swayed a bit then came back to the subject.

"D'ye know that heid-banger Pally McComb?"

I nodded.

"Well, I heard it was Wullie Morrison that ran ower ma dug. So I gave Pally a couple o' rabbits tae gie him a doin'. I wid have done it masel but I didny want involved wi' the law." His voice sank confidentially. "As ye know I huvny got a dug licence. Anyway, Pally is that shortsighted that he didny know the difference between Wullie and Johnny, so he banged Johnny."

"I see," I said, but I didn't think it was such a great story.

"How's the dug then?"

"I selt it."

"Ye selt it?"

"Aye, it wis gettin' past it. Matter o' fact it wis a bloody nuisance wi' a' these complaints aboot it. But dae ye know who I selt it tae?"

"Naw."

He began to laugh then went into paroxysms of

14

coughing. I was getting impatient. He finally calmed down.

"It wis Wullie Morrison that bought it."

I said nothing. I couldn't make any sense out of it.

"Ye see," McDonald wiped the tears from his eyes, "I sent Pally up wi' a note tae Wullie this afternoon tae say he'd better buy the dug, due tae its poor condition efter bein' run ower, or else. Well, he must have seen the state o' his brother's face, so he sent the money doon right away. Mind ye, I didny think he'd gie me twenty pound. Personally I'd have settled for a fiver."

"Wullie could never stick the thought o' pain," I said. I began to laugh as well, and hoped Paddy would keep on his feet long enough to get me another drink.

"Right enough, Paddy," I said, holding firmly on to him, "ye're a great case, an' I'll personally see that when ye kick the bucket ye'll get a big stane above yer grave, me bein' in the buildin' trade an' that."

2

I was taking a slow amble along the river bank. The weather was fine, one of those spring mornings that should gladden anyone's heart. The birds were singing, the trees were budding and the fishing season had started, but I was feeling lousy. The scar in my temple and the cuts round my mouth were nipping like first degree burns. My neck felt like a bit of hose pipe and the lump on the back of my head was so tender that even the slightest breeze lifting my hair made me wince. My mother's remark, "You look like Frankenstein", had not been conducive to social mixing, but since I wanted someone to talk to I decided to look up my old china Paddy McDonald because at times he could be an understanding man if he was not too full of the jungle juice.

I turned with the bend in the river and there on the bank, under the old wooden bridge, was a gathering of his cronies, namely, Billy Brown, Big Mick, Baldy Patterson and Craw Young. They were huddled round a large flat stone that displayed two bottles of

Eldorado wine and some cans of beer, but I could not see Paddy.

They did not hear or see me approaching. Billy Brown jumped up as startled as a March hare when I asked, "Where's Paddy?" at the same time staring hopefully at the wine.

"Paddy's deid," he informed me.

My brain could scarcely adjust itself to this statement.

"That canny be true." Without waiting for the offer I took a swig from the bottle.

"It's true right enough," replied Billy, smartly grabbing it back. "I found him masel up in the Drive as cauld as ice an' as blue as Ian Paisley."

The Drive was a derelict building where the boys did their drinking when it was too cold for outdoors.

"Whit happened to yer face?" asked Big Mick.

"That's a long story." I was so stunned by the news that I had forgotten about my face for the first time since I woke up. Billy wiped his mouth with the back of his hand. His eyes were like saucers and his face greyer than grey. He was a close associate of Paddy's. Not exactly a mate, more like a sparring partner, but they spent a lot of time together except when they were in jail.

"I didny know whit tae dae, so I got the polis in an' they sent for an ambulance. They carted him off while I waited ootside."

"How dae ye know he wis deid? When Paddy wis out cold he always looked deid," I said.

"If ye'd seen the colour o' his face you'd hiv known he wis deid." No one disputed this fact.

"That wis a rerr wee hoose he had," said Baldy Patterson wistfully. He was referring to the broken-

17

down bothy where Paddy lived. "I think I'll go up efter an' see tae his pigeons."

"That's great," I said. "The man's hardly cauld an' ye're gaun tae move in."

"He wis cauld enough when I seen him," said Billy. "Onyway, somebody has tae feed his pigeons."

The second bottle was opened and passed around with some beer, and now I was included in the company. Normally I don't care for wine and beer first thing in the morning, but this day was an exception what with my sore face and Paddy being dead. Now that I was hunkered down on eye level with them they began to study me.

"Yer face has improved a lot since I last saw ye," said Craw Young who always fancied himself as a bit of a wit. "Ye've got a bit o' character in it noo."

"Better watch I don't put a bit o' character in yours," I retorted, but I didn't put any emphasis on my words because they were all away beyond my age group and fragile with years of steady drinking and sleeping out. I thought Paddy had been the toughest despite his burst ulcers and periodical fits if he was off the drink for more than a week, but I was wrong. Mellowed by the wine and the sadness of Paddy's death, I explained how five fellows from the city had picked a fight with me and stuck broken tumblers in my face. It was really only two fellows but I had my reputation to think of.

"It's the bad company ye keep," said Billy sagely. "We auld chaps know the score."

"Is that so," I said, "an' jist how many times have you been in jail?"

"Och, that's only for disturbin' the peace and vagrancy. Ye canny count that."

"Anyway, Paddy must have been OK this mornin' if

18

he was in the Drive, otherwise how wid he manage tae get there."

"He got lifted last night wi' the polis as far as I heard, but they must have let him oot early. I didny get in tae the Drive till aboot eleven this mornin'," explained Billy.

"Where were you last night then?" asked Big Mick with suspicion.

"I don't mind much aboot last night," said Billy sheepishly. "Matter of fact I woke up in Meg Brannigan's."

We all jeered. Meg Brannigan was a slattern who drank anything from Vordo to meths. Even Billy was a cut above her.

"Anyway I jist happened to pass oot on her couch."

We jeered again.

"Here," said Craw who had been deep in thought. "How d'ye know it wisny murder?"

"It wid be murder bein' wi' Meg," chortled Big Mick.

"I mean how d'ye know Paddy wisny murdered?"

"I never murdered him onyway," said Billy vehemently.

"OK, OK," said Baldy, "the main thing is whether he wis murdered or no' who's gaun tae bury him?"

"Bury him?" we echoed.

"He's got tae be buried an' don't forget that'll cost money."

We looked at each other with dismay.

"He'll jist have tae go intae a pauper's grave," said Craw with a lack of taste.

"Terrible tae think o' poor Paddy in a pauper's grave," said Baldy.

"It'll no' dae him ony harm. He'll have plenty company."

"Maybe he wis insured," said Big Mick.

"Nae chance," said Billy. "He discussed it wi' me once. The insurance company wid have nothin' tae dae wi' him. He's whit ye call a bad risk."

"Maybe we could get up a collection," said Baldy.

"Who the hell is gaun tae put tae it. Who dae we know that's got money. I mean real money."

My face was feeling painful again and I was fed up with all this debate. Paddy had been the only one with any smattering of intelligence about him. Now he was gone.

"Anither thing," said Big Mick. "We'll have tae let the priest know."

"First I heard Paddy wis a Catholic," said Craw sharply. He turned to Baldy, "Did you know that?"

"Naw, but I always thought there wis somethin' funny aboot him."

"He didny tell me onyway," said Craw bitterly, "for he knew ma opinion aboot Catholics."

"I never knew you had opinions aboot anything," said Big Mick. I could see he was becoming angry. Likely he was a Catholic too with a name like Mick.

"Anyway," Billy Brown butted in, "you don't even know whit you are. You telt me ye wir an orphan."

"I might've been an orphan but I wisny a Catholic."

"Who cares?" I said.

We all glared at each other for some seconds. Then to prove how displeased he was with the subject Big Mick finished off the remainder of the wine in one swallow. We stared gloomily at the empty bottle.

"I'm off," said Mick with the air of a man who is going to get things done. He threw the bottle into the river and marched off with as much determination as his long shaky legs would allow him.

I said, "Me too." Groggily I arose, wishing I had gone to work. It couldn't have been any worse.

After the evening meal of sausages and mash, one of my mother's favourite dishes, I sat staring glassily at the television. I didn't particularly wish to venture into the Paxton Arms to meet types like Willie Morrison. He would be overjoyed at the brilliance of my savage face and even more so at the news of Paddy's departure. After all, he had been so terrified of Paddy he was forced to buy his dog, and Willie hated that dog, though he was too frightened to get rid of it. And that dog, for all its mean look, had a loving nature. It trailed on Willie's heels like a shadow. Willie would dodge up closes to avoid it, but to no avail. It could always seek him out panting and slavering with joy. With Paddy gone the dog was definitely a goner too. My mother sat down to view the telly twitching about and straightening cushions. I suspected my company was a bit of a strain for her. I said, "Did ye know that Paddy McDonald is deid?"

"Is he?" she replied in a flat voice. We both stared at the box. Finally she said, "He'll no' be much loss anyway."

"I suppose not." I kept my voice neutral.

"He wis nothin' but a tinker anyway," she added.

"There wis nae proof he wis a tinker."

"He wis worse. He wis just a drunken auld sod that neither worked nor wanted."

I let the remark go. I could not expect her to have any understanding of Paddy.

"By the way," I said, "I heard he wis a Catholic. If he just died this mornin' when wid they haud his mass?"

"Usually the same night, I think."

"Whit time aboot?"

"Maybe seven. I mind that's when they held mass for Mrs Murphy." Then looking aghast she added, "Don't tell me ye're gaun tae the chapel for that auld rotter."

"Don't be daft," I said, but inwardly I thought I should. It would be the decent thing to do. I was feeling a bit emotional about it all, and stood up quickly before she noticed my eyes were wet.

"I'm away oot," I said before any more remarks could be made.

I headed for the chapel with a lot of indecision. It's right next door to the boozer which is handy for the Catholic voter. I noticed there was more business going for the chapel though. You would have thought there was free beer by the manner in which everyone rushed up the stairs. I hung about until the rush was over and looked up and down the street furtively. Which was it to be, the boozer or the chapel. Then I thought, what the hell, I should pay my respects to Paddy. I took the plunge and scurried up the stairs. I didn't know what I expected to see behind these dreaded doors, but apart from a couple of statues and something that looked like a fancy washhand basin, there was nothing much to put me off.

I sneaked in through another door to be confronted with all the solemnity of the papal worship. My face was red as I squeezed into a bench at the back because all the seats were jam-packed. But not a soul bothered or even gave me a glance so engrossed were they in the sermon. The priest's voice was a meaningless drone to me, and I wondered if the mass for Paddy had begun. After a time I felt relaxed enough to look around at the decor. I considered it quite tasteful and if anything, except for the odd statue here and there, quite plain. I liked that. It was peaceful and uplifting. Maybe Paddy's death had a meaning for me. Maybe it was to join this mob and get a bit of religion. Definitely food for thought. Though it would be fine if I could hear what the priest was saying, but whatever it was it would be appropriate and Paddy would be pleased if he could hear. Probably he could. In this place anything was possible. Then it struck me I couldn't see Paddy's coffin. Perhaps it was too early for this. I wished I knew more about these matters. To see if it was lying handy I stood up. An old woman sitting next to me whispered as loud as a shout. "Sit doon son. It's no' time for staunin'."

I sat down quickly. No sooner had I sat when everyone stood up. For the next half-hour we were up and down like yo-yos. Though you didn't sit all the time you were down. Sometimes you had to kneel on the long stool on the floor. I was beginning to get the hang of it but it was very sore on the knees. Still there was no sign of Paddy's coffin, nor had I heard a mention of his name. At one of the sitting parts I whispered to the old woman next to me. "Could ye tell me missus if the priest is saying mass for Paddy McDonald."

I don't know if the message got through but her reply made no sense.

"Look," she said balefully, "I don't know anything aboot Paddy McDonald, but whatever they tell you I've lived a decent life for the past ten years and atoned for everything. I'm never away from this bloody place atoning — so don't start."

Her voice finished on a hysterical note. All eyes that

had been transfixed forwards were now transfixed backwards on me. The priest, as distant as a postage stamp picture, had stopped swinging the smoky stuff. I was so burnt up with embarrassment I felt my wounds were opening up to drip blood. I wiped my face on an ancient paper hanky but sweat only dampened it. Then the pressure was released. The eyes turned away and the priest carried on swinging the smoky stuff. I had scarcely got over all this when, out of the blue, everyone got up from their seats and began to walk down the aisle in a single file, even the old woman. I couldn't stand any more so I stood up as though I was going to join the queue but instead turned quickly to the right, out of the door, passing the fancy washhand basin and into the marvellous fresh air. It was the only sensible thing I had done all day.

The first person I bumped into, or rather he bumped into me, was Paddy McDonald. I wasn't all that surprised. The absence of his coffin or any mention of his name had cast doubts anyway. I didn't want to know him now. He was in one of his complicated, mindless moods. In other words, completely stoned. He clung to me as if I was a long-lost lamp-post. If he had been sober there were a million questions I could have asked him, but as it was I merely said, "Hi Paddy."

Stoned though he was he was bursting with information. "D'ye know whit I'm gaun tae tell ye?"

"Whit?" I said.

"Because o' that stupid sod Billy Broon I wis carted off tae hospital this mornin'. They widny let me oot. Telt me ma liver was a' tae hell. It took me a' day tae get ma haunds on ma clathes." He paused to regain the drift of his conversation, still gripping me tightly. "Noo they tell me that Billy an' the team are in ma hoose lettin' a' the pigeons away an' God knows whit else. Wait till I get ma haunds on the bastards."

I tried to break from his vice-like grip, saying, "Ye'd better hurry hame then before they set yer hoose on fire."

In his agitation he released me. Facing the Catholic church he uttered every blasphemy he knew. It seemed to me that Catholics are a very extreme lot. If they are not one way they are the other. Of course that is only my opinion. In the middle of it all I walked away. Though I hoped he had the energy to batter Billy Brown to a pulp for the bother he had caused me. And all this had to happen when I had a sore face.

3

"Any old rags! Toys for rags! Any old rags!"
The voice of Duds Smith, magnified through an old tin trumpet, roared up our street, penetrating the thickest eardrum.

"I wid jist as soon burn ma rags than gie them tae that auld cheat," said my mother in her usual arrogant style.

"I thought ye usually wore them," I muttered.

"Whit's that?"

"Nothing." I then added the uppermost thought in my mind, "How's about a pound till Friday?"

"Don't be daft. For a' the money you gie me I couldny afford nothing."

She went on to explain at great length that I must be unaware of the fact the cost of living had risen in the past five years and surely I must realise the fiver I gave her every week would hardly keep a dog going. Fixedly I stared out of the window. I knew she would eventually wear herself out then begin to feel guilty at my lack of defence. At the least I might get fifty pence from her which was the entrance fee for the Paxton

Arms. Her tirade petered out and she sat down breathing heavily while Duds's voice penetrated the pregnant silence. His motor was now opposite our window. Kids were running out with bundles large and small leaving a trail of scruffy articles behind them while Duds was handing out balloons and Hong Kong whistles in a benevolent style and deftly slapping to the side any of them who were returning burst balloons and soundless whistles.

"Mean auld swine," said my mother as she joined me to survey the scene. I knew she was playing for time.

"Here, I tell ye whit," she said suddenly excited, "gie Duds that auld telly lyin' in the bedroom an' ye can take a pound aff the money ye get."

"Don't make me laugh!" I allowed the flicker of a smile to crease my face which was just beginning to heal from the broken tumbler episode. "Ye'd have tae pay him tae take that telly away. It must be the original one Baird invented."

"It could be fixed easy. Ye can still get a picture."

"I'll tell ye whit," I said, not wishing to waste time on the merits of the television, "I'll take the telly doon tae him if you gie me a pound for tryin', whether he takes it or no'."

"OK," she said.

Duds was not thrilled when I laid it down on the pavement. My arms were almost wrenched from their sockets with the weight.

"Look Mac, I've more televisions in ma back yard than auld lawnmowers."

"Maybe," I gasped for breath. "But this one still works."

He stared at it in disbelief.

I explained, "Ye see, we've got a new telly, so ma mother wants rid o' this one, but if ye don't want it I'll take it doon tae auld Mrs McMurtry. She said she would gie us a fiver for it, that is if ye could oblige me wi' a lift roon tae her hoose."

Duds was convinced. "I'll gie ye two pounds for it."

"It's a deal," I said.

I told my mother, "Duds only gave me a pound."

"Is that all?"

"Ye were lucky even tae get that."

"Have I tae get the pound then?" she asked hopefully.

I became indignant at the way she was trying to get out of her deal. "C'mon, ye said ye'd gie me a pound if I got rid o' it or no', so I keep the pound an' you've saved a pound."

"I gie up," was her final comment.

Later on I was enjoying my pint of beer in the Paxton Arms and having a friendly chat with Flossie the barman, when in came Willie Morrison, down in the mouth as usual, and not enhanced by a piece of sticking plaster decorating his chin.

"Did ye manage oot withoot yer dug then?" I asked.

Willie looked over his shoulder nervously, "I don't know where that animal has got tae. Took it oot for a walk the other night an' the bloody thing jist disappeared."

"Better watch the farmer disny catch it worryin' the sheep, an' shoot it."

"I hope no'," he said brightening slightly.

"Still, Paddy McDonald wid be terrible disappointed if it wis shot," I pointed out.

"I'm past caring whit Paddy McDonald thinks, or any o' his damned relatives."

I wondered what the relatives had to do with anything.

I changed the subject. "Did ye cut yer face shavin'?"

"Naw, did you?" he replied, giving my face a keen look.

"Maybe." My face was healing but I had to keep it poker straight or the cuts near my mouth would open up.

"Whit are ye wantin' tae drink then?"

I was surprised. Willie is not famed for these kind of impulses.

"A hauf an' a hauf pint," I answered quickly.

He gave the order without a blink and said, "It's a terrible thing when a fella canny take a drink withoot somebody wantin' tae pick on him."

"Did somebody pick a fight wi' ye?" I asked dutifully and fingered one of the fifty pences in my pocket wondering how I could avoid wasting some of it on Willie.

He replied, "Ye know Murdo McDonald?"

"Ye mean Paddy's nephew?"

"Aye. One's as bad as the other."

I nodded. I had gone off Paddy myself.

"Well, he gave me a punch for nothin'."

"Did ye no' punch him back?"

"I don't believe in punch-ups. I charged him but he got aff wi' it."

"I'm no' surprised. I've seen more damage wi' a midge bite."

"There's jist nae justice in the world," Willie moaned.

He was beginning to weary me. I decided to inform

him about my financial position. "I'm sorry I canny return the drink. I've only enough here for one pint."

Willie shrugged like a man who is used to disappointments.

Just then the subject of discussion, Murdo McDonald, and another rat-faced fellow joined us. I nodded over to Murdo. I had nothing against him. He was a volatile, quick-tempered type with a strong sense of fair play. He stood close to Willie with his pitted face almost touching Willie's. Willie shrank visibly.

"Er — would ye like a drink?" he asked Murdo.

"Sure thing. Make it a double whisky an' one for ma mate."

Hastily Willie ordered two doubles. "That's me skint," he mumbled after he paid. Nobody answered. He swallowed a remaining mouthful of beer and made a sheepish exit from our company. The coast was clear. With my fifty pence I ordered a whisky and beer for myself.

"That wee scunner wid make ye sick," said Murdo inclining his head towards Willie's back disappearing through the door.

"How's that then?"

"He wis cheatin' at cards the other week, so I punched him. No' much. Jist opened up his face a wee bit. The next thing he had me charged wi' grievous bodily harm. I warned him wi' ma haunds roon' his neck I wid gie him real grievous bodily harm if he didny withdraw his statement. Well, anyway, the case came up yesterday. When the magistrate asked him tae point oot the accused, meanin' me, Willie said he didny know who punched him. I thought you said it was the accused here, said the magistrate, meanin' me. Willie said he didny know who it wis, but it definitely wasn't the accused, meanin' me. The magistrate wis that fed up wi' him he fined him a fiver for contempt o' court."

I refrained from laughing for obvious reasons. Murdo did not laugh either because being the great avenger that he is, he has no sense of humour and the rat-faced mate likely had heard it all before. With the remainder of my two pounds I ordered a drink all round.

For the rest of the evening I was kept going in beer by Murdo and his mate who were glad of an audience. My head was swimming in a mild haze of alcohol, nothing extreme, but quite enjoyable for through the week when you don't expect much. As a further bonus, at closing time Murdo ordered a carryout of a half-bottle of whisky and cans of beer. He then asked me if I'd like to pay Paddy a visit along with him and his mate. "Sure," I said without hesitation. "I think Paddy's a great case."

In fine spirits the three of us tramped up to Paddy's place. Over the boggy fields, skirting the farm, down the lane plastered with cows' dung, past the stinking byre, cheerfully assuring each other that the smell was good for us, until we reached the moss-covered dwelling of Paddy's. A pig might have turned up its nose at this hovel, but when our senses were blunted we enjoyed its homeliness. Without knocking we marched straight in and found Paddy lost in the magic world of television. I could hardly take my eyes off it. Paddy barely glanced in our direction.

"C'mon Paddy. Get the glasses oot. We're havin' a party," said Murdo.

What was uppermost in my mind was that this

television was the one I'd sold Duds. My mother was right. It went fine, and to think I'd only got two pounds for it. The drink was dumped on the table, which was really a wooden crate covered in flowery plastic material. The cat was knocked off the sofa by Murdo to allow us to rest on the exposed springs, but we were all feeling deflated by Paddy's lack of enthusiasm. Finally he had the decency to say, "Jist haud on a sec till this programme's finished. It's great."

We all stared at Kojak's hairless face. I can take Kojak or leave him, but right now I preferred to leave him. However, it finished off with the usual farewell speech to a dishy bit stuff, then thankfully we turned to the plastic bag with the drink.

"Right Paddy, get the jeely jars oot. We came tae see you, no' watch the telly."

Reluctantly Paddy turned it off. He removed the plastic cover to reveal an impressive display of stained glasses inside the wooden crate, no doubt owned originally by the Paxton Arms.

"Help yersels lads, but jist drink the beer oot the can. It'll save me washin' up later."

Murdo poured a big measure of whisky for Paddy. It must have shot straight into his bloodstream for he brightened up right away like a flash bulb.

"How did the case go, son?" he asked Murdo.

"Fine. I got aff."

"I should think so. Fancy anyone accusin' Murdo o' grievous bodily harm. A nicer fella ye couldny meet," appealed Paddy.

Rat-face and me stared sympathetically at Murdo's pitted face.

"Ye're right there Paddy," I said. "By the way, how did ye manage tae get a telly?"

"It wis Murdo here that got me it."

I looked enquiringly at Murdo.

"Ach, it wis nae bother."

"It's a fine telly. Who selt ye it?" I asked.

He laughed, which was unusual for him. "Folk don't sell me things. They gie me them. Anyway, I'll tell ye whit happened. Ye know that twister Duds Smith, the ragman? Well, I happened tae be hingin' aboot when a wee laddie gave him a great bundle o' rags. Duds gave him a balloon that widny even blaw up. The laddie wis greetin' so I telt him tae get me a breid knife, if he had one in the hoose. He brought me a great carving knife. I showed it tae Duds. I telt him if he didny gie the boy somethin' better than a balloon I wid gie him the knife — right in the ribs. So Duds gave me this telly. I kept the telly and gave the laddie ten pence."

"You're a decent fella Murdo," said Paddy.

Murdo bowed his head to hide his embarrassment.

Rat-face said, "So ye urr."

I drained my beer from the can and said nothing.

4

The other Saturday I met up with one of my old schoolmates, Toly McGee. I think his correct name was Bobby, or it might have been Rabbie, but I always knew him as Toly on account of one or two accidents he had in the classroom. In those days he had a very nervous disposition. I gave him a genuine "how's it gaun" welcome and noticed he hadn't altered that much. The big brainy forehead wrinkled in perplexity as he peered at me with the same flickering eyes of old. They slowed down to a standstill when recognition dawned on him.

"It's yourself," he said with such a great grin of pleasure I wondered if he really knew me. He shook my hand with hot enthusiasm and I had difficulty in ungluing it from his clammy grasp. I was beginning to regret my impulsive greeting because I could see I'd have difficulty in getting away from him and I was in a hurry to put a bet on.

"Huvny seen ye for a while," I remarked.

"I've been in England since I left school," he told me.

I thought that explained the posh accent. "Did ye run away?" I asked.

"Of course not! Mum and Dad left for London with the family. You remember Dad?"

I remembered Dad. He used to be "the auld man" to Toly. He was a shuffly, ferrety-faced wee guy who worked on the railway and, when drunk, battered Toly stupid.

"Right enough," I said, "I remember ye a' lit oot for the big smoke."

Vaguely it came to me that the talk with my mother at the time was the McGees had done a moonlight after getting free passes on the train. It also struck me that Toly was dressed neatly in a brown suit with tie to match, and a crew-cut which did not enhance his naked face. It wasn't my idea of style. Still, there was an air of success about him compared to the old days when he wore his father's shirts with cuffs turned up a mile, ragged trousers which barely reached his ankles, and either wellies or sandshoes regardless of weather conditions. I could sense he was about to embark on a long conversation so I cut him short.

"I'll huv tae get this bet on before the one-thirty race," I explained and smartly headed across the road to the bookie.

"That's alright. I'll wait for you," he called.

"Jesus," I muttered. I hung on till after the race, but my luck was out. The horse had been lame, and Toly was waiting.

"It's really great to see you again," he said for the umpteenth time as we walked along the road. I knew I was lumbered with him, and for his part he didn't notice my lack of interest in his life story.

"So, anyway," he said, "after I got the money I

thought I would return and look up my old friends."

"Whit money?" I asked, jerked out of my apathy.

Impatiently he said, "I've already explained about the money Dad won on the pools. He gave me two hundred pounds to start me off in business, but I thought I would come back and have a holiday in my home town first. I've told you all this already."

"Sorry," I said, "wi' that fancy accent o' yours I couldny follow whit ye were telling me. Anyway, I'm glad tae hear aboot yer good luck. I like tae see folk gettin' on."

Although I'm not a grasping type I was relieved that Toly at least possessed money to splash about.

"Do ye take a bevvy?" I asked cautiously.

"Bevvy? Oh, I see. Yes, I don't mind an occasional pint. In fact," he added with genuine pleasure, "I would be glad to treat you."

I breathed a sigh of relief because if Toly didn't indulge I would have dumped him there and then. Hurriedly I invited him into the Paxton Arms, since there was only an hour's drinking time left. Toly ordered the beer and with our pint tumblers before us, we stood like two clothes poles waiting for a line.

Eventually I said, "I don't care a' that much for the taste o' beer withoot a whisky tae go wi' it."

Toly took the hint. He ordered two whiskies. His face went a fine shade of lilac after he swallowed his, but it must have put some sense into him because after shuddering he said, "Don't worry, I'll buy you all the whisky you want."

"That's very decent o' ye Toly."

He regarded me uneasily and said, "I'd prefer if you didn't call me that name. Do you mind addressing me as Robert."

I gave a bark of laughter, "That's a helluva name. Toly suits ye better."

His eyes fluttered with embarrassment. "In Tolworth they call me Robert. No one has said it doesn't suit me."

I felt sorry for him, so I said, "So ye stay in Tolworth? That's the game. I'll call ye Tolworth. I'd forget tae call ye Robert, but Tolworth sounds like Toly. How's that?"

He brooded a bit then conceded, "I suppose so."

I slapped him on the back. "Right Tolworth, I'll have a hauf an' a pint."

After another couple of rounds he began to sag inside his neat suit. I thought he looked all the better for it. His tie flapping at the side of his neck gave him a touch of class and more in keeping with the Paxton Arms style.

Not having much to talk about we began to reminisce on the subject of our schooldays. Tolworth confessed that he had detested school.

"You wereny the only one," I said.

"It wis different for you." I noticed he was relapsing into the vernacular of his race. "You didny seem to bother aboot beatin' ups." Then he gave my face a long look. "I see you still don't bother."

"I bothered the same as everybody else," I said. "Ye jist had tae put on a front."

"Aye, but ye didny have to put on your faither's auld shirts that made you a handy target." His voice was bitter.

"That's true," I admitted. I never had a father so I had better fitted shirts from the welfare.

"By the way," I said, "there wis one thing that puzzled me aboot you."

"What?"

"Well, mind how we used tae come whoopin' an' shoutin' oot o' the class at playtime?"

"Aye."

"It wisny as if I wis spyin' on ye, but it began tae dawn on me that efter ye came whoopin' an' shoutin' the same as everybody else, ye disappeared intae thin air. One day I wanted tae ask ye for the len' o' yer sandshoes for drill but I couldny find ye anywhere."

Tolworth looked at the glass of whisky in his hand sadly. I could sense there was a big confession coming.

"I widny tell anyone else but you," he hesitated, then continued. "As you know I've always been very allergic to pain, on account of gettin' battered from ma auld man when he was drunk. Ma bones were always that sore that I couldny stand any shovin' or punchin', and nobody wid play wi' me anyway. So I used to run straight oot and wait inside the toilet till the bell rang."

I looked at him with genuine compassion. Imagine standing for fifteen good playtime minutes in the toilet, waiting for the bell to ring to get back to the torture. I put my hand on his shoulder as a measure of my sympathy. "Ye've had a terrible life," I said when he ordered another two glasses. He began to unburden himself even further.

"Do you know, many's a time I was standing at the school gate at seven in the morning."

I was aghast. "I always thought ye were brainy but I didny think ye were that keen on school."

"It wisny that," he said with such an air of tragedy that I was dreading what he was going to say. "You see, ma auld man sometimes sat up a' night drinkin'. He hudny a clue whit the time was. He would stagger through to ma room to get me up for school and if I

38

didny get up he would pull the blankets aff and pour
cauld water over me. It wis better to wait at the gates,
even in the winter, than argue wi' him."

I felt a lump in my throat. Tolworth blew his nose on
a spotless white handkerchief saying in a matter-of-fact
way, "Oh well, that's the way the cookie crumbles."

At this point I ordered two whiskies, being the
decent thing to do in the circumstances. After that
everything became fuzzy. Whatever we discussed or
how I got home I don't know, but the next apparent
event was my mother shaking me hard and bawling in
my ear, "There's a fella wantin' tae speak tae ye."

I sat up, surprised to see I was in bed. I tried to pull
myself together.

"Whit's the time. Is it Sunday?"

"It's half-past four, and it's still Saturday."

Thankfully I lay back. The evening was still ahead of
me untouched.

"D'ye hear whit I'm sayin'? There's a fella wantin'
tae speak tae ye. Strikes me as bein' one o' these
queers."

My mother had queers on the brain due to a recent
television play. Even I was under suspicion.

I said, "Tell him tae beat it."

"Tell him yersel. He's waitin' in the living room."

In a stinking mood I stumbled out of bed. It was
Tolworth awaiting. There wasn't much resemblance to
the neatly dressed fellow I had first met. There were
more creases in his suit than a concertina. His shirt
hung outside his trousers and there was no sign of a tie.
He clutched me by the vest and said in a sickening
whine, "You'll have to help me. There's a mob after
me. I don't know what to do."

My mother viewed the scene with arms folded and

nodding her head as if her worst expectations had been confirmed. "Who's this then?" she challenged.

I explained that he was Tolworth McGee alias Toly. Surprise and recognition softened her. She asked, "How're ye keepin' and how's yer mither an' faither?"

In between the snivelling Toly replied, "Fine," then returned to the snivelling. My mother became bored with the lack of information and said, "I'll pit on the tea."

"For God's sake, pull yersel the gither," I said when she had gone into the kitchenette. "Whit happened?"

"I don't know whit happened. After you left I think somebody picked an argument wi' me. I threw a glass o' beer in his face. The next thing I was ootside and a gang was chasin' me. I managed to get away." He added with a touch of pride, "I wis always good at runnin'."

"Whit dae ye want me tae dae?" I asked.

"Can you no' help me?"

"Listen chum, I'm no' gaun tae spoil a good Saturday protectin' you."

My mother entered with two cups of tea and a plate of banana sandwiches.

"Ye've excelled yersel," I said looking darkly at the meal.

Ignoring the comment she addressed Toly, "Mind an' tell yer folks I wis askin' for them."

"Sure, I can hardly wait," he mumbled, drawing the cup shakily up to his mouth.

The tea must have revived Toly a bit for he said, "If only I could get to the railway station I would be OK but these guys might be waitin' for me."

"I'll tell ye whit," I said with inspiration, "we'll wrap yer haund in bandages then we'll put yer arm in a sling.

40

Nobody will touch ye then, an' I'll take ye tae the station."

Toly was doubtful, but I had the feeling if I didn't get him out of the house right now he would stay forever, like a refugee in hiding, and my mother would be glad to keep him as company for her old age.

My mother was annoyed at the sight of one of her sheets being torn up for bandages, but as she must have felt sorry for Toly she assisted in making him appear a pathetic casualty. She waved a cheerful hand out the window as I prodded him along the road. Sure enough, further on the way, two of the Hoodlum Gang were leaning against the fence. I gripped Toly's arm hard to keep him from running away.

"Whit a horrible sight," sneered one of the gang.

"Look," I explained, "he's already had a doin' an' broke his wrist. So there's nae need tae gie him anither one."

"That's right," said Toly with a ghastly ingratiating grin. With wooden faces they stared at him. One stabbed a knife into the fence. Toly gasped. Hurriedly we moved on When I looked back the knife was still being stabbed. But anyway we reached the station and I left Toly on the platform, ignoring his plea to wait with him. I had done my duty and the Paxton Arms would be open. I was in the pub for only half an hour when my mother marched right up to the bar beside me. I was surprised. She wouldn't enter a lounge let alone a public bar. She explained, with a face like flintstone, that Toly was back in the house with a genuine broken wrist waiting on the ambulance.

Sure enough, when we got back Toly was lying on the couch at the end of a trail of bandages beginning from the outside door, and bellowing like a bull.

41

"Whit's happened noo?" I asked, tempted to damage him further.

He stopped his noise long enough to tell me that the two Hoodlums had followed him to the station. "I showed them my wrist, telling them it was broken."

"We already telt them that," I said with irritation, adding, "so, whit did they dae?"

Toly sobbed. "They must be monsters. They kicked it six times."

He carried on sobbing until the ambulance came.

During the next few days my mother visited him in hospital, taking in grapes and bananas. Then she told me she was thinking of giving him a holiday when he came out because the McGees had been awful nice folk. She asked me if I would mind giving Toly my bed and I could sleep on the couch, assuring me it was quite comfortable. This morning they let Toly out and I was waiting at the hospital gates in a taxi. I reminded him that the Hoodlum Gang never forget, so in order to make a quick getaway before they got on his trail again he could take the taxi to the railway station. He was very grateful, and we parted the best of mates.

5

I could scarcely believe my eyes when I came home early the other day from work to see Proctor Mallion drinking tea with my mother. His round, shiny face was unusually benign, though tinged with embarrassment, when he said to me, "Hullo son." My mother glared at me as she said, "You're hame early."

I shook my wet tammy over the table. "I got rained aff," I said, and snapped, "hurry up wi' the dinner."

I turned on the telly and sat with my eyes glued to Bugs Bunny in order to avoid looking at Proctor. Drunk, he was a psycho case, sober he appeared a smarmy greaseball. He finished his tea off with a noisy slosh, "I'm jist away."

"Aye, ye'd better hurry. The pubs have been open for a full five minutes," I shouted after him.

The sausages and mash were dumped with a bang before me.

"When's the wedding?" I asked.

"Don't be so bloody sarcastic. Just because I gave the man a drap o' tea ye needny try tae make something o' it."

"I don't want tae see that man in this hoose," I said.

"So, it's your hoose now."

I tried being reasonable. "Look, that man's a nut case. He'll come back here when he's drunk an' smash the place."

"As far as I'm concerned it's a case of the pot calling the kettle black," said my mother coldly.

I could see it was useless. "I'm away tae bed for a rest."

"Aye, only till the pub gets busy."

Later on I ran into Paddy McDonald in the Paxton, quite sober. I told him about Proctor Mallion drinking tea with my mother.

"Tea?" he echoed.

"That's beside the point. I got the impression he was courtin' the auld wife."

Paddy shook his head. "Never," he said. Paddy is very courteous as far as women are concerned. I don't think he ever had much to do with them. He told me, "Yon's a bad one, and no' the type any woman should take up wi'. His first wife ran away wi' the insurance man and his second wife left him efter he pushed her oot the windae. Lucky for her it wis on the ground floor."

"The worst o' it is," I continued, "I canny lay a finger on him or she'll turn against me."

"D'ye want me tae lay into him?" asked Paddy.

If Paddy had been a hard man there were not many signs left. Years of steady drinking had worn him away nearly to skin and bone.

"Thanks Paddy, but better leave it."

"You could always slip Pally McComb a fiver tae dae him. Pally's a good hatchet-man," said Paddy.

"I widny waste ma money on Pally. Proctor would floor him wi' a glare. It's no' Willie Morrison ye're dealing wi'. Naw," I added thoughtfully, "it's got tae be something subtle."

"Look," said Paddy, "there's Proctor comin' in."

I looked to see him staggering up to the bar, staring with unfocused eyes around him, likely looking for someone to latch on to. He zig-zagged towards us, then crashed into a chair. Flossie, the barman, emerged from his hideaway and glared at Proctor with hands on hips. Ineffectually he had barred Proctor on a number of occasions, but Proctor either ignored or never remembered them. Flossie, a peace lover at heart, usually forgot he had barred Proctor until he got the current bouncer to throw him out again. Bouncers in the Paxton Arms ran the same hazards as deputy sheriffs so it was never the same guy twice that dealt with Proctor. I could see that Flossie was trying to make his mind up whether to call on the latest bouncer who was happily playing darts impervious to the disturbance. I was trying to make my mind up whether to leave. Proctor was slowed up by the chair, but he headed towards us with drunken determination. Then he did some intricate steps as one foot tripped over the other and fell flat on his face. Flossie's mind was made up, "Benny!" he shrieked in the direction of the dartboard, "get this pest out."

Benny threw a dart wildly at the board and approached Proctor.

He hauled him up to a standing position, gave him a kick on the legs, then threw him backwards through the swinging door.

"To think," I said despairingly to Paddy, "that's the auld wife's fancy man. Maybe my future stepfaither."

"Ran into yer boyfriend," I informed my mother when I returned home at the early hour of nine o'clock.

"Who's that then?" she asked keeping her eyes on the telly.

"That lovable bundle of fun, Proctor Mallion."

"Ye've got a nasty tongue on ye."

"It's nothin' compared tae yer boyfriend's. When I last seen him he wis gettin' flung through the doors o' the Paxton. Still, he might take a look in later, provided he husny got picked up wi' the police."

Her answer was to turn up the telly very loud.

"Get the tea on!" I commanded, thoroughly incensed by everything.

"Get it on yersel! Ye're big an' ugly enough."

I regarded her with distaste. With her frizzy hair and torn tights Proctor might be the best she could get. I supposed it wasn't much of a life watching the telly and the occasional bit of gossip for entertainment. Pity moved me into the kitchenette wherein I prepared a pot of tea and some slices of toast. She wasn't impressed when I handed her my offering.

"Wonders will never cease," she uttered, pointedly breaking off a black bit crust.

I tried again, "Whit's for tomorrow's pieces, an' I'll make them masel. It'll save ye gettin' up in the mornin'."

"Spam," she said, then, "are ye sure ye're feelin' alright?"

As I buttered my eight slices of bread I reflected it was going to be hard wakening myself. Still, if this soft soap was applied long enough she might consider it better to have me than Proctor in the house, because it would have to be one or the other.

"Goodnight," I said to her before I retired. I tried to

add the word "mother" but since we seldom addressed each other by our names it was difficult. She didn't even answer, so engrossed was she in the telly.

Everything went wrong in the morning. First of all I slept in. I had to leave without tea. On the site I discovered the bread I had buttered was minus the spam. The wall I built collapsed because the ganger insisted I use wet brick. "Get ma books ready, I'm packing it in!" I told the foreman.

"Away hame an' tell me tomorrow," he said. I returned home about three in the afternoon to find Proctor drinking tea and eating cheese sandwiches. I grabbed him by his greasy collar and ran him out the door. "Come back here an' ye're oot the windae the same as yer last wife!" was my message.

My mother's mouth was still open from shock when I came back into the living room. "And don't think I don't mean it!" I said.

I entered my bedroom and lay down feeling exhausted but unable to sleep because of the rage that tore at my head. But I must have dozed off because I woke with a start at the sound of a tray being dumped on the coffee table. I knew I had to begin again. I didn't feel like it, but I must get rid of Proctor once and for all.

"Sorry about the carry on," I mumbled as she wiped spilled tea off the table with one of my nearly new vests.

"Think nothing of it," she sneered throwing the vest violently onto the bed.

"Tell ye what," I said, "how's aboot comin' wi' me into the Paxton lounge for a wee break. I'll buy ye a sherry."

"I don't drink," she replied through clenched teeth. But somewhere I must have struck a chord for she added, "Anyway, I might gie ye a showin' up. I've nothin' much tae put on."

Inwardly I conceded that could be true. I said, "Put on that nice fur coat ye got frae the Oxfam an' ye'll be lovely. In fact I'll introduce ye tae a real gentleman compared tae which Proctor Mallion looks like a bit shit on the pavement."

I didn't add that the gentleman was Paddy McDonald. She must have been impressed for she said, "Anything tae keep ye happy."

We sat in an obscure seat at the back of the public bar, although my mother was under the impression she was in the lounge, and I did not disillusion her. Self-consciously she patted her frizzy hair fresh from the curling tongs. I hoped no one would mistake her for a girlfriend. Doubtfully she informed me she would have a sherry. As I ordered the bevvy Paddy entered. I was glad to see that he was miserably sober.

"Do me a favour," I asked him, "I want ye tae meet the auld wife. She's sittin' back there."

He looked round furtively, but said courteously, "An' a fine lookin' woman tae. I'm surprised ye don't bring her here mair often."

"Are ye kiddin'? Listen, I'm trying tae get rid o' Proctor Mallion, an' this is all part o' the set-up. Have a word wi' her an' prove there's better fish in the sea."

He was aghast. "Ye're no' suggestin' I should start courtin' her?"

Actually I hadn't considered this. Paddy would have been as unwelcome a stepfather as Proctor. "Nothin' like that," I assured him, "jist come an' sit at the table for a while tae take the bad look aff us." Reluctantly Paddy brought over his beer.

"Meet Paddy McDonald," I said in the way of introduction.

My mother turned pink. I was surprised considering the contempt she had for him. Stiffly Paddy seated himself, also looking flushed. I thought this was going to be great. The two of them acting like teenagers.

"Very pleased to meet you," he said.

Her face lit up. "It's a pleasure I'm sure."

After the second sherry my mother relaxed and addressed herself exclusively to Paddy. He was listening avidly to her every word. I gave up all pretence at listening because, apart from the fact that I was bored to tears, I spied Proctor Mallion at the bar arguing with Flossie. The upshot was that Flossie conveyed the message to him loudly, "Listen sonny boy, YOU are barred!" Proctor's answer was to hurl a glass through the mirror behind the bar. Flossie screamed and ran for cover. My mother gave a moan of fear. This excited Paddy's chivalrous instincts. He hurried up to Proctor and smashed a lemonade bottle on the counter over his head. Immediately my mother gathered up her coat and ran out the bar shouting, "That's the last time I come oot wi' you."

As it was to early for a bouncer to be on the scene, impulsively I took on the job myself. I'm not all that keen on a fight but if there's one set out handy before me I have no alternative but to take part. Besides, Paddy was about to be executed any minute. Proctor, whose skull must have been as thick as concrete, was rising to his feet with bared teeth. Neatly I tripped him up, at the same time instructing Paddy to beat it quick. After I put the boot in on Proctor once or twice he was out for the count, and it was easy to deposit him on the pavement. The police van, which is as regular as a good taxi service, cleaned him off and all was quiet again. Flossie was grateful. He asked if I would like a job as a bouncer. "Naw, but I'll have a double whisky."

When I returned home my mother was watching the telly as usual.

"Some carry on that wis," she said. "Ye'll no' catch me in one o' these lounges again."

"It was a' your fault anyway."

She was amazed, "My fault!"

"If it hudny been for the fact that ye were encouragin' Proctor Mallion I wouldny have taken ye to the Paxton. I thought ye must be havin' a right dreary time when ye took up wi' a character like him."

She appeared to be so stunned that she became breathless. Finally she said, "Me, takin' up wi' Proctor! The only reason he was in the hoose wis because I wis sellin' him that set o' tools lyin' under yer bed. They've been lyin' there for ages an' I could never get cleanin' the room right because o' them. I only got a fiver but it was well worth it tae get rid o' them."

"Wait a minute," I said, scarcely able to credit my ears. "You didny gie him ma set o' tools that took me two years tae pay up when I wis an apprentice brickie?"

"Well, ye never had them oot the box as far as I can remember."

"Ye don't understand," I said slowly, my head beginning to ache. "Ye never use yer own tools if ye can help it. Ye always nick somebody elses. If ye took yer own tools they wid jist get nicked."

She was unperturbed. "How should I know that?" Then she had the cheek to add, "How's aboot makin' a cup o' tea?"

"Get lost!" I replied.

50

6

Come this particular Saturday, a day I normally look forward to with great enthusiasm, I lost interest in the usual programme. Maybe I was becoming too aware of increasing pressures. All Friday night's talk had seemed loaded to me. Usually discussions go above my head unless I'm personally involved, but phrases like "Are ye lookin' for trouble", "Stick the heid on him" or "He's only a Tim" pierced through my ears and stuck in my brain until, for no apparent reason to anyone, I threw a glass at the mirror behind the bar.

"Bouncer!" shrieked Flossie.

I walked out voluntarily to save any bother. So here I was on Saturday morning heading for a bus to take me to the splendours of the west away from alcoholic fumes and unreliable moods.

Collie Lumsden and a mate were sitting on the wall at the bus stance. Collie used to work beside me on the building sites until he gave it all up to be a full-time alcoholic.

"Where are ye gaun?" he called.

I replied, "Up country." At present I was not on the same wavelength as him and did not fancy his company. To cover up I asked civilly, "Waitin' for the boozer tae open?"

He nodded then offered me a can of lager. Collie always took it for granted everyone was gasping for a drink. Usually he was right. Reluctantly I took the can, wishing the bus would hurry before I was sucked back into my familiar social life.

"That's an idea," he said with inspiration. He turned to his mate, "We'll get the bus up tae the Clansman. It should be open by the time we get there." I was fed up. I could see how things were going.

Luckily his mate replied, "Don't be daft. You are barred in the Clansman."

Collie was incredulous. "For Christ's sake, when wis I barred?"

"Dae ye no' mind dancin' on tap o' the table when ye wir last there. Then they pit ye oot."

"Christ," repeated Collie, dismayed, "I don't mind that. Maybe ye're right."

The bus moved into the stance. Thankfully I got on, and bumped into a big fella who was getting on at the same time. He stood back apologetically but not before I nearly choked on a mouthful of his long hair. I don't mind long hair but this was ridiculous. It almost reached his waist. I gave him a cool stare as I quickly scrambled aboard. Then with a wave to Collie and his mate I settled down to view the fresh pastures flying past.

By the time I reached my destination I was squeamish. The bus had been stuffy and the road had possessed the structure of a scenic railway. I tottered off wondering whether to head for the Clansman, but I forced myself to give it a miss. Instead I purchased a bottle of lemonade and a pie then headed for the pier and a boat alongside. A chalked board informed me that the mailboat was due to leave any minute for passengers wishing a trip round the islands for fifty pence. This was worth a try, so I climbed aboard. There were some sightseers on deck with the loud English patter. I hunched into a corner and the wooden rails dug uncomfortably into my shoulder blades. Seconds before the boat moved off the big fella with the long hair climbed on. Our eyes met with the awareness that one lonely type has for another in closed company. But I turned my head to convey the message that if I was alone I liked it that way. I made up my mind there and then I was getting off at the first island. I had no intention of being trapped on this boat for any length of time with these foreigners.

"Going off already?" asked the highland boatman, pocketing my fifty pence and no suggestion of change when I conveyed my wish to him.

"Aye, if ye don't mind."

"Not at all son, we'll catch you on the way back," he said as though I was a fish.

Ignoring his helping hand, I leapt onto the jetty of an unknown island. I nearly fell in the drink, but desperation saved me. Like a fugitive I scurried up the first path which led me away from the shore. I sensed contemplative stares following me, but when I turned round the moon faces on the boat were becoming harmless dots. Only the big fella stood out like a well-drawn sketch. I retreated into the under-growth.

The path carried on through woods, ferns and streams. I was feeling great now, like Chief Chingach-gook. The path began to lead upwards over the top of the island. It was hard going hauling myself up over bits of rock and slippery earth, but it was worth it when I reached the top. Panting and sweating, I lay down on the bracken to get my breath back. The view was terrific, all lochs and mountains. I felt contempt for my mates who would be firmly established in the boozer by now, slugging away at whisky and beer, unaware that there were better ways of passing the time. Yes, this was the life. I brought out my pie and lemonade. The pie was squashed and the lemonade lukewarm, but it was the most enjoyable meal I had eaten for a long time. I took off my jacket to make a pillow. With the droning of the bees and the heat of the sun on me like an electric blanket, I fell sound asleep on my bracken bed.

I don't know how long I slept but the heat had faded and I was stiff and thirsty. I shivered as I took the last swig of lemonade. Shakily I arose and followed the path downwards into a wood. But it was still great I assured myself. I started to sing, "I love to go a-wandering", but the sound of my voice was so unnatural I changed it to a whistle. I wished I could see a wee furry animal, or even a deer. That would be something, but I appeared to be the only animal that was moving. Or was I — I wondered. I could hear the noise of branches breaking now and then, and there were rustlings in the bushes. I hoped it was one of these wee furry animals, or likely it was a bird.

"Come oot, come oot, whoever ye are," I shouted recklessly. No one answered right enough, which made it worse. I began to walk quickly, then ended up running. I don't know why, but once you start running it makes it a certainty that somebody's following you. Then I saw the loch looming through the trees. I reached the open space of the shore. I slowed down. The panic was over. The sun switched on again and a speedboat streaking along the horizon was reassuring. I sat on a bit of rock and looked over the water. Now I thought it was a pity there was no one to talk to. But it was even more of a pity I hadn't brought a half bottle of something to calm the nerves. Still, I wasn't used to walking about islands and staring at lochs. I must concentrate on how great it all was. I looked hard at the loch for ten minutes until I had to admit that I was just fed up. I began to get a thirst and it wasn't for water, so I started moving again.

I followed the path deeper into the wood fighting through ferns which were as tall as myself. It was getting harder to follow the path and I was beginning to think I would never get out of this jungle when I emerged at last into a clear grassy bit where the trail led upwards again. I could be heading back to the jetty, the escape route to civilisation and the Clansman. Then I spied the top of a building on another path to the left. I thought I might as well investigate this while I was here.

The building turned out to be merely a hut, neatly boarded up and of no earthly interest, but beyond that was the entrance to a graveyard. It was a very wee graveyard and very old. The gravestones were a dirty dark grey and standing at all angles. A perfect background for Dracula. I studied one big stone closely and could make out a fancy design with words written underneath, "Here Lies the Corpse of Jessie Buchanan". On another there was a cheerful verse which I managed to decipher after peering at it for five minutes:

> Here Lies Tom,
> His Life was Squandered,
> His Days are Done,
> But Yours are Numbered.

In the middle of all this creepiness was a wooden seat twisted and gnarled as a corpse itself. I could picture Tom of an evening coming out of his grave and sitting there peacefully with arms folded and legs crossed. So I sat down too. It was strange but I couldn't hear any birds singing now. The only sound was my breathing and I tried to quieten this down a bit. I sat as still as the vision I had of old Tom because I didn't think I could move even if I tried. I had the crazy feeling I was part of the seat. Then from the wood there was a crack as if someone or something had stood on a branch while he or it was watching me. I could bear it no longer. I wrenched myself off the seat and ran past the hut down the path then up over the top of the island like a mountain goat. I didn't stop until I reached the jetty, just in time to be caught by the mailboat returning.

Once I got my breath back I noticed everybody had loosened up since I last saw them. They gave me broad, forgiving smiles for leaving. I smiled back gratefully because at least they were human, if English. "I'll take the High Road and you'll take the Low" they sang to me with big winks. "An' I'll be in the pub afore ye" I rendered back as quick as a flash. This caused a laugh all round. The big fella still stood apart looking at me calmly as if he had planned it all. Anyway all this did not matter because the boat was chugging towards the mainland and the Clansman.

Beneath the plastic beams and cross swords of the Clansman I downed my beer in one gulp. In the bar there was only myself, the barman and a tweedy type in the corner, of no consequence. The barman wasn't much cop either. Pointedly he wiped a spot of beer on the counter, spilled from my glass. "Lively," I thought. Then I became aware of a looming presence behind me. I turned to encounter the gentle blue eyes of the big fella.

"Could you tell me, pleaze," he asked in the exact English of the educated foreigner, "how I ask for some beer and spirits?"

"Sure. Ye jist say a hauf an' a hauf pint."

"Zank you." He turned to the barman, "A hoff and hoff pint."

The barman was puzzled. "What's that?"

"A hauf an' a hauf pint," I explained.

"That is what I say," said the big fella.

"Aye, but it's no' whit ye say, it's the way that ye say it."

"Beg pardon." His voice was uncomplaining.

I sighed. I become bored when I have problems in making myself understood.

As if he knew what I was thinking he said, "I hope you shall speak with me. All this day I have been alone and now I think it would be pleasant to speak with someone."

I looked steadily at my beer so he could not read the annoyance in my eyes.

"Speak away chum."

"Chum?" he questioned.

"Mate then."

"Mate?"

I sighed, "Friend then. Savvy — friend?"

His big face creased into a beautiful big smile.

"Friend — that is good. You will be my friend."

I could see it was going to be hard to shake this guy off. Maybe he was a nut case. It was hard to tell with foreigners. For them and us there would always be something lost in the translation. I looked him over. His gear was casual but expensive, down to the open sandals. Leather, definitely not plastic. Probably a foreign hippy. One of the flower people. All love and marijuana. Though he looked familiar, as if I had met him before. But I wasn't happy with his company. He was not my style. He swallowed his whisky with the ease of a professional drinker. Then I thought maybe he wasn't so bad.

"Whit's yer name?" I asked.

He understood this. "Max." He held out his hand. His grip was warm and firm.

"Call me Mac. Everybody does," I told him, with no hope of understanding.

He laughed. "Mac and Max. It is the same. Perhaps we are the same."

Privately I didn't think so, but I agreed. "Sure," then, "you're a Gerry, I mean a German?"

His face straightened. "Yes, but I would prefer to be Scottish."

"How's that then? I mean why do you prefer to be Scottish?"

"In Scotland everyone is kind. In Germany they are not kind. All they wish to do is work and make money.

They do not care about people. In Scotland people do not have this wish to work and make money all the time. If they have enough they are satisfied. Here people have helped me and many times buy me whisky. Sometimes they speak loud and violent but I think they have kind hearts."

It did cross my mind that he might be a con man, but still I did not wish to disillusion him about our kind hearts, so I ordered two whiskies.

"Pleaze," he protested, "I will buy you a whisky." He carefully extracted a fifty pence piece from a leather purse.

The barman frowned, "Another ten pence," he snapped.

To save time I quickly slapped down the ten pence. At this point the big fella brought out a parcel from his stylish anorak and laid it on the counter. Fascinated the barman and I watched as he unfolded it to reveal sandwiches and a hard-boiled egg. He offered us both a sandwich and then started to unshell the egg. I accepted mine gratefully but the barman refused his. He seemed to be searching for words. Unpleasant ones I suspected.

"Do you have castles in this place?" the big fella asked him.

The barman was defeated. Without answering he walked away. Maybe to look up a rule book, consult his union or 'phone the police.

"Whit dae ye want wi' castles?" I asked.

"I have come here to study Scottish castles," he explained as though it was as normal as cleaning windows. "Then I shall write my book. I shall send you a copy since you are my friend. I shall have it specially translated."

"Whit dae ye want tae dae that for?" I asked, returning to my original opinion that he was a nut case.

"Because you are my friend."

This guy definitely had the knack of making a fella feel self-conscious. To change the subject I said, "You remind me o' somebody."

He considered then replied, "I understand. I remind you of Jesus Christ," without as much as a smile. I was convinced, definitely a nut case.

He went on, "In Germany many people say I look like Christ. I have been asked to take this part in the Passion Play, but I refused because I do not like to pretend."

He offered me his last sandwich. I declined. My appetite was gone. I was not certain, but the sandwich could be a test. He shrugged and ate it.

"My friend," he said, "I would willingly buy another whisky, but I have only a little money, just enough to buy a ticket on a ship to return home."

That figures, I thought. "Don't worry I'm gaun for the bus anyway."

"Good, I must get the bus also."

It all loomed up. Back home to the auld wife with Max. She would love him. He would have my bed and I would have the couch. Quickly I ordered a carry-out leaving the barman wiping crumbs off the counter with a pained expression on his face. When we were seated on the bus I handed him a can of beer. The old dames in front gave us cold stares. He didn't notice. I didn't care. For me it was always the done thing. The booze had no affect on him. My head was feeling swimmy but I was resigned. The big fella was coming home. I was not going to be the one who turned him away.

Again he read me for he said, "I have a room to go to this evening. As you call it, a bed breakfast place."

With relief I said, "That will cost you plenty. Ye can always get a kip, I mean a bed, in ma hoose. Ma mother is a great person. She will put anybody up for the night." I took care to look away as I said this.

"This woman is also good. She does not charge much money, because she explained I must stay in the kitchen since I might upset the guests."

I was indignant. "Jesus Christ!" I blushed at the expression, "that's terrible. How could ye upset the guests?"

"My hair is very long as you see. Sometimes it is upsetting to others. In Germany when people drink too much they wish to cut my hair off. For this reason I did not go out at night."

I was disappointed at this gutless attitude so I forgot to look away.

"You may think," he explained as though I had said so, "that I was afraid, but I do not believe in violence. Many times in the past I gave my parents much sorrow. Once I was a drug addict." At least I had guessed that correctly. "But with their love they helped to cure me so I keep my hair long that I will remember my disgrace. It is my penance."

He looked at me intently. "In your face I see the scars of violence. Perhaps that is your penance."

I said nothing. He was wrong. I liked my scars. They were status for me. The bus drew in at the terminus. We got off. Everybody rushed away, maybe glad to escape from his loud, open conversation, and we were left alone. In a last attempt to do the right thing I said, "Are ye sure ye'll not meet me later? We could have a drink the gither."

He placed a hand on my shoulder, "This would not be wise. For you my presence would cause violence because you are my friend, but give me your address so that I can send you my book."

I wrote my address down on the back of my bus ticket. He placed it carefully in a wee book.

"How can ye be so sure of everything?" I asked. "I mean that ye'll even get it published."

"I am sure," he replied with his awful certainty. He tucked his hair neatly inside his polo-neck jumper, shook my hand then walked away.

I looked after him wishing I could be as sure of everything. I turned the corner to head for home, kip, then tea and the boozer. Outside my close two lassies were skipping to the chant of

> "Old King Billy has a ten foot willie,
>   He gave it to the lady next door,
>   She thought it was a snake
>   And hit it with a rake,
>   Now it's only nine feet four."

Trust the papes to know all the good ones. "D'ye want a kick in the backside?" I asked them.

"King Billy! King Billy!" they shouted, then ran away laughing.

They are a right ignorant lot round here, but some day I will get away from this place. Some day I might go and see castles myself.

7

The modern trend was catching up with the clientele of the Paxton Arms. For the first time in living memory we were going to have entertainment. Behind the bar, cellotaped to the mirror, was a poster informing us in bold black print that a group called the Basket Weavers were, at great expense to the management, making a personal appearance every Friday at 8 p.m. We, the regulars, were suspicious of this development because, being creatures of habit, we always expected to have the same conversations and the same arguments with the same faces.

"Once they start bringin" groups in here it'll never be the same," pronounced Paddy McDonald. "A' these microphones an' amplifiers will only deafen us an' droon oot the conversation."

"Too bloody true," agreed Splash Healey, spraying Paddy with beer as he spoke.

Paddy wiped his face and considered, "Still, it might serve a purpose. Some folks are better keepin' their face shut."

Now though Splash was one of the most affable and generous of fellas nobody could stick his company too long. He was usually left alone at the end of an evening swaying about the bar talking to himself or his dog. Even the dog didn't pay too much attention to him. It was always sprawled sound asleep in front of the bar, causing folk to trip over it every time they went up for a glass of something. Not that he was excluded completely from our company, because as I said he was generous when he had the cash. Many a time he kept me going in drink through the week when I was stuck for the ready, though my discussions with him were limited and usually confined to pats on the back to both he and his dog. Speaking of his dog, I knew it well. It had been Paddy McDonald's before it became Willie Morrison's, and it had taken a lot of effort on Willie's part to convince it that it was not wanted — like trying to brain it with boulders. Splash had came across it one night in a dazed condition. Being a kind hearted fella he had adopted it on the spot. It turned out to be a suitable arrangement since the two of them had a lot in common.

However, to get back to the subject of the group, when Friday came we were all in the Paxton as usual. Despite our prejudice about entertainers we were curious about them. It must have been about half-past eight before they appeared, and by then we had forgotten about them and were getting involved in deep discussions. Twice Paddy had tripped over Splash's dog and what was worse he had spilled his drink the second time.

"That bloody dug wants drooned," he said, giving it a kick. The dog opened one eye. If it remembered

Paddy from away back it gave no sign. It just growled and shut its eye again.

"Sorry aboot that Paddy," spluttered Splash. "I'll get ye anither drink."

"Aye, well watch it then," said Paddy. He added, "I never thought tae see the day when an animal wid put a man aff his drink — here, whit the hell is that?"

A noise like a balloon letting out air exploded in our ears.

"It's only the group testing," explained Flossie nervously.

We turned to see what was going on and there was the group testing their gear and tossing their hair about.

"Whit a racket," groaned Paddy, "if that's whit it's gaun tae be like I'll be givin' this place the go-bye."

"That we should be so lucky," gushed Flossie.

"Gie the fellas a chance. They're only testin'," I said.

"Aye, they're only testin'," repeated Splash.

"Sounds mair like they're testin' their arses," said Paddy tersely. However, sensing that opinion was against him he kept quiet.

After coughing and repeating the word "testing" for ten minutes the group finally got going. They gave us *A Boy Named Sue* and *A Girl Called Lou* which went down great and got loud cheers from everybody except Paddy who was staring moodily at his empty glass. He had been trying to attract Flossie's eye for a while, without success, since Flossie was giving all his rapturous attention to the group. He was recalled to reality when Paddy threw a box of matches, hitting him on the nose. But Paddy's views had lost their impact. By now we were all livened by the beat and thought the group were great. Eventually they stopped to refresh themselves and we were plunged into comparative silence.

"That wis rerr," said Splash with enthusiasm and straightaway ordered three pints for the group to show his appreciation.

"Ma heid is fair nippin' me," said Paddy, "I think ma eardrums are burst."

"Gie us a break an' stop yer moanin'," I said, and moved away to have a word with Joe Duffy, a workmate on the site. If Paddy did not appreciate good music that was his hard luck. Big Joe and I spoke for a time about the work in general and the ganger in particular. Suddenly Joe broke off his discussion to say, "Will ye look at that eejit?"

I turned to see Splash gripping the mike and prancing up and down in a silent mime of Al Jolson.

"Put that mike down!" yelled Flossie, "ye'll break it."

"He's doin' a lot better than the other bampots anyway," Paddy declared. "At least he disny make as much noise."

This triggered off fellow feeling for Splash. "C'mon Splash — sing up! Gie us A Four-Legged Friend," someone shouted. This was the song Splash usually sang outside the pub at closing time as his four-legged friend walked away in disgust. Splash did not need much encouragement. He never had it so good. He began in a screechy tone "A four-legged friend, a four-legged friend—" He broke off. "Naw, wait a minute, that's too high," and began again, "A four-legged friend, a four-legged friend," in a deep bass. "Naw, wait a minute, that's too low."

The audience was enchanted and falling all over the place with laughter. Then someone shouted,

"Get aff!" Another one shouted, "Gie the fella a chance!"

Splash tried again, "He'll never let you dow-en," in the right pitch for shouting "coal". Being satisfied he carried on. The microphone must have been saturated. Apart from the cracking of Splash's voice it was making cracking sounds of its own.

All this did not pass unnoticed by the group. They tried to laugh it off at first. Then they quickly finished their beer.

"OK, that's enough. You've had your fun," said one of them. He tried to disentangle Splash from the mike, but Splash was glued, and he carried on like the true trouper, "He's honest and faithful right up to the end—". The group member relinquished his hold. Likely he thought it was the last verse. When Splash started on another he lost his head.

"Gie's a haund wi' this nut," he called to his mates, and they all began struggling with Splash. Bravely he held out encouraged by the audience shouting, "Let the fella alone!", "Ya big cowards!", "Pit the heid in Splash!". Even the dog, awakened by his master's voice, gave threatening snarls. I was surprised when Big Joe, normally a level-headed fella, rushed up with great fire to pull two of them away and grab the third by his psychedelic tie, almost throttling him. After a temporary surprise the group pulled itself together and made a combined onslaught on Joe, knocking him to the ground and putting the boot in with a lot of determination. Pandemonium broke out. Glasses were hurtled indiscriminately in the direction of the group and anyone near at hand. Beer was poured over Splash to quieten him down as he still continued to belt out the four-legged friend, and Flossie beat a hasty retreat into the back premises. I noticed one or two old scores which were nothing to do with the present matter being settled. My loyalties were divided. I thought Splash had it coming, but at the same time I felt bound to give Joe a hand. Just as I reached out to grab a chunk of hair there was a restraining grip on my arm. It was Paddy's. "I telt ye groups wir nae use in a bar. Leave it. The polis will sort oot this lot. They'll sort ye oot as well if ye interfere."

Paddy was usually right in a lot of things so we retreated into a corner to await the final crunch. It didn't happen because three regular bouncers with three volunteer bouncers took care of the situation. The group, defeated by sheer numbers, were pushed out into the world beyond with their equipment crashing behind them. Everyone simmered down except Splash who burst into tears.

The night wore on. Drinks were set up. I seemed to be losing the power of speech and movement. This happens to me once in a while. I fell asleep over the table. When I woke up my back felt as curved as a hoola-hoop. Where is everybody I wondered. I lifted my head and tried to get everything into focus. I swivelled my eyes and managed to contact Splash slumped over a table to the left and Paddy drinking beer sitting at a table to the right. Ahead of me Flossie was listlessly moving a cloth over pools of liquid on the counter. The Indians must have attacked again for the mirror behind the bar was smashed for the umpteenth time.

"Whit happened?" I croaked. "Where is everybody?"

"Away hame," answered Paddy, "an' it's time we wir as well."

"Get us a drink." I knew if I could even get a short one I would feel better.

"Bar's closed!" Flossie informed me with relish.

"Listen bum-boy," said Paddy, "get the lad a drink afore I beat ye to a pulp."

I sensed Paddy had undergone a lot of pressure while I was sleeping it off. Flossie shrugged his shoulders. Insults hardly touched him. He put two whiskies on the counter and I noticed no money was passed. I gulped my whisky and felt a fraction better. Splash's dog sat up alert and ready for anything now that everyone was gone. It padded around, sniffing here and there then finally peed up against a chair. Flossie ventured the message, "Do ye no' think it's time ye were away."

"I'll go when I'm good an' ready," said Paddy.

Splash was beginning to surface. He lifted his face to the ceiling and began on the four-legged friend again.

"Gie Splash a drink as well," demanded Paddy.

Flossie banged another whisky on the counter. "I canny take much more o' this," he said.

"Look Paddy," I said, "Flossie is right. Ye'll only get the polis in."

"Don't worry," said Flossie, "the polis will no' touch *him*." He put a lot of emphasis on the word "him".

"Whit dae ye mean by that?" I asked.

Flossie's face twitched. Paddy said nothing.

When Splash began to sing again after swallowing his drink Flossie's control ran out. "The polis don't touch Paddy these days. He's an informer."

"Is that right?" I asked Paddy.

"Maybe." He changed the subject as if it was of no consequence.

"Dae ye want anither drink?"

"There's no chance of that," said Flossie, and continued with abandon, "he thinks because he's in wi' the polis he can dae whit he likes. See when you wir sleepin' the group came back, but they wir hardly in the door when they were lifted. I saw Paddy gie one o' the polis a wee nod. He thought I never noticed."

"Let's hope naebody notices this," said Paddy. He drew the back of his hand off Flossie's cheek, causing a trickle of blood to ooze from the barman's nose. Flossie began to whimper.

"Is that true," I asked, "that ye're an informer?"

Paddy shrugged. "Think whit ye like. That's a good word 'informer', but I'll gie ye better ones. How aboot 'psychiatry treatment'. How wid ye like these words thrown at ye every time ye come up in dock. They say, 'Just once mair Paddy — or else'."

"Or else whit?"

"Christ's sake, dae I have tae draw ye a diagram?" He went into a brooding world of his own and finally muttered, "I want tae die in my ain hoose. No' in jail or hospital."

"Ye mean yer ain midden," I sneered.

"Call it that if ye like."

It appeared as if he had answered my question. I regarded Splash who had returned to the senseless stage. I shook him viciously.

"C'mon, get up," I said, "ye're gaun hame. You and yer dug."

He yelled as I hauled him up by the skin of his shoulder. "Where are we gaun?"

"Hame — wi' me."

Splash was the last person I wanted to take home, but I was filled with a twistedness that wanted to do the awkward thing.

"How's that?" he asked, spitting over me as usual.

There was nothing better to say than, "Because ye're a better man than he is Gunga Din," jerking my head in Paddy's direction.

Flossie had dried his eyes by this time and was handing Paddy another whisky. I walked past them both without a word. Splash lurched behind me with his dog following. The night air must have nipped my eyes because they were wet, and I had the cheek to talk about Splash being a wet guy, but then if ever I had liked a fella it had been Paddy and him an informer.

8

"Whit's happened tae that wee layabout Rab Tunnock?" the ganger asked me in an aggrieved tone.

"How should I know," I replied as I wiped the mortar off my trowel.

"Well, ye might know if he has been in the pub recently."

"Never seen him." I turned my back and placed a brick with marked concentration.

"If ye dae — tell him he's paid aff."

I carefully evened off the mortar and said nothing. I wasn't going to be the one to do the ganger's dirty work. I had seen Rab the night before lying stupefied on the grass outside the Paxton Arms, but what had happened to him since was anybody's guess. Besides, at the moment I didn't give a damn about anything. My hands were stiff and my feet were numb. It was a damp, freezing morning. My jacket, bought in the height of the summer, was as warm as a piece of net and my year-old boots were as sturdy as a pair of sandshoes. In the summer you completely forgot about the winter so when it came you were never prepared. You just wondered how you could wangle a sick line. But if you did go on the sick you hated every minute of it, being exposed to the heavy breathing of the auld wife bitter about money prospects. Who would work on a building site, the worst trade in the world in the winter? Talk about the miners. At least they had Mick McGahey. The nearest we ever got to a strike was one from a winey's spade. Anyway who could protect us from the sleet and the frost? Then we had to put up with gangers like Harry McCafferty who must have served his apprenticeship in Siberia, intolerant of anything above a twenty-five-watt bulb in the workmen's hut and a nip of alcohol to put a bit of heat in you.

McCafferty walked away. "Whit's the time?" I asked the apprentice.

He looked at his digital watch. "Half-past eleven."

"Dear Christ, another hauf 'oor tae go. Ma fingers will have fell aff by then."

"Mine as well."

"How's that? Ye've had them in your pockets a' mornin'. Look lively, we'll never make oor bonus at this rate."

He glared at me then picked up his trowel. Right enough he was a knockout. The first wall he had built collapsed as he was admiring it. Luckily the wind blew it away from him instead of on top of him.

"Always lock yer hut before ye leave in case the tools get stolen," I had told him. He had done that, never bothering about who was in it. After shouting themselves hoarse McCafferty and the foreman had managed to unpick the lock to free themselves.

However, he was now McCafferty's blue-eyed boy because he never drank, never took a day off and never answered back. He never did much work either.

Eventually the whistle blew. We all stamped into the hut.

"It's bloody freezin' in here," we complained.

"Whit aboot gettin' us a heater? We're fed up strikin' matches," said Fitty Peters to McCafferty who was munching away on his sandwiches.

"You lot don't work hard enough to get the circulation going," said McCafferty. We ignored this statement and chewed on our pieces.

"Another thing," he said, "ye don't eat the right grub. Whit's that muck ye've got?" he asked me.

"Spam," I replied.

"Ye're lucky," said Fitty, "I've got jam."

"I've got roast pork and pickles," said the apprentice.

"It's a' rubbish," pronounced McCafferty. "The best thing for keepin' oot the cauld is a flask o' soup followed by broon breid an' peanut butter sandwiches.'

"Imagine that," said Randy Smith, "a flask. We couldny afford one."

"Naw," said McCafferty, "but ye can afford tae staun in the pub a' weekend."

"That's how we canny afford a flask," I said. "It's a vicious circle."

"Anyway," said Big Joe to McCafferty, "if I lived like you I'd hang masel, but we're no' interested in yer diet. We want a heater or else we don't work."

"Is that whit ye call it — work?" said McCafferty. "Well, if ye don't work ye're paid aff, so please yersels." He gave a righteous belch then marched out.

"Maybe he's away for a heater," said Randy wiping the drips from his nose.

"Mair likely away for a shit," said Fitty.

"He hasny a good one in him."

The apprentice turned red. "Don't talk dirty in front o' the boy," laughed Randy.

I stepped out of the hut to throw away a tea bag. "Will you credit that," I shouted, "it's rainin'!"

"Good, we canny work then. Get the cards oot."

We put ten pence each in the kitty. I dealt the cards. We played in silence, apart from the odd curse. After losing two games the apprentice said he was fed up and threw in his hand. We played some more. Then Fitty said, "I've nae money left, unless somebody wid like tae pay me in."

"No thanks," we all said.

So far I had won fifty pence when McCafferty returned. "OK boys, time's up — oot!"

"Whit do ye mean?" we asked. "It's rainin'. We don't work in the rain."

McCafferty exploded. "It's only drizzlin'. Ye don't work in the cauld! Ye don't work in the rain! Who dae ye think ye are — a bunch o' bloody civil servants!"

"We don't work in the rain," Big Joe repeated and proceeded to deal out the cards.

McCafferty swore. "You mollycoddled bastards! This job is away behind schedule as it is. Every day somethin' happens wi' you lot."

"Like last week when auld Jimmy broke his leg fallin' through a hole that wis covered up wi' sackin'," I said.

"It wisny covered wi' sackin'," growled McCafferty. "He wis half blind wi' booze."

"Ye needny worry aboot bein' behind wi' the

schedule," said Big Joe, "because ye've saved this firm a lot o' money in compensation wi' a' these accidents ye swore were pure carelessness."

"I'm no' gaun tae bandy words wi' you lot. Just get back tae work or ye're a' paid aff."

The apprentice stood up and placed himself beside McCafferty.

"Right!" said McCafferty when he saw we were unmoved, "ye're a' paid aff except the apprentice here."

The apprentice was now outside the hut. We carried on with the cards.

"That's it then," said McCafferty, and banged the door behind him.

At this point we threw our hands in. Randy put the cards in his pocket. "Might as well take them hame."

"Oh well," said Big Joe stretching himself, "I could dae wi' a week or two in front o' the fire."

"Aye, but it's no' so good when ye've nae money," said Fitty.

"We're OK for the weekend anway. Who's worrying aboot the future?" I said with bravado.

"There's always the supplementary," Big Joe reminded us.

"Aye, efter six weeks."

I was beginning to get depressed. "How aboot runnin' doon tae the licensed for a bottle of wine?" I asked Fitty. "I'll pay for it. I've just got enough."

"That's a good idea," said Randy. "I'm no' that keen on gaun hame. The wife'll no' be exactly overjoyed."

There was a general agreement. Fitty returned with the wine and we poured out a measure into our mugs. We started to play cards again. This time it was for matches — not much of an incentive. Now a bottle of wine might be an average drink for one but between four it does not last long, and finally we were pouring it out in minute measures. The talk ran out and the game became boring. The bottle was drained and flung in the bucket. Then the door opened and McCafferty said, "I telt ye all. Ye're sacked! There's nae point in hingin' on."

"Get stuffed!" said Big Joe.

McCafferty turned away. "Well, ye'll have tae go hame sometime."

We sat in silence for about three minutes. "This place is as cheerful as a mortuary," said Big Joe. "I'm away hame."

"I'll have a drag before I go," said Randy. He brought out his shag and handed us each a roll-up. My eyes were nipping. I closed them to ease the tiredness. When I opened them I was alone. I lit the roll-up and lifted the bottle from the bucket to drain the dregs, feeling cold and hopeless but reluctant to move. The aftermath of being paid off was always the same. I tried to recall how many times this had happened. Perhaps I never should have been a brickie. I had always fancied myself as a joiner. Once I spent a fortnight converting a set of drawers into a bookcase. It hadn't been a success, but I always had the yearning. When the Youth Employment sent me to Smeddon's Building Contractors, the foreman had said, "We don't need apprentice joiners, but a big lad like you would do well as a brickie."

"No thanks," I had said.

"You might change your mind. You've got a great build for a brickie. Come back tomorrow if you do."

My mother had told me to get back up the road to Smeddon's. "Ye'll no' get another chance," she said.

"I don't want tae be a brickie," I had shouted as I banged my fist on the wall, but the next day I returned to Smeddon's and become an apprentice brickie. I carried the hod, laid common brick, facing brick and coping stones. I laid brick down manholes and laid brick up ten storeys, but I never had a pound in my pocket beyond a Monday unless I won it at cards. I was twenty-two. My arms were knotted like a man of forty-two, and sometimes my back ached as if I was fifty-two. And it all added up to being paid off once again. Oh well, there was no point in feeling sorry for myself. I might as well get a bit of shut-eye before I returned home to break the glad tidings. I eased myself up onto the bench and tried to forget it all.

I woke up freezing, and had to stamp up and down in the hut to get the circulation going. I opened the door. It was grey fog, so I shut it quick. There was nothing to hang around for, but it was funny to think I would never see these four wooden walls again, or that naked pin-up above the kettle, or that Carlsberg Special ashtray stolen from the boozer. I was getting that feeling of foreboding which strikes me now and again like a clammy hand on the shoulder. For Christ's sake, I thought, I'm only twenty-two with no real problems, but sometimes I could see myself winding up on the river bank like the wineys, with all my possessions in a plastic bag. Let me kick the bucket before I reach that stage was the nearest I ever got to a prayer.

"Are you there McCafferty?" a voice roared in relief to my thoughts.

The door burst open and there was Rab Tunnock

stoned out of his mind brandishing a brick hammer. He aimed it at the side of the hut.

"Calm doon," I said.

"Calm doon! That bastard McCafferty has paid me aff!"

"We're a' paid aff, so forget it."

"Bastards!" he said.

He lurched over to the wall and pulled the brick hammer out and swung it round his head. He was a terrible spectacle. Oaths spewed from him like the bile as his eyeballs swung in harmony with the hammer. If my sympathies were not for McCafferty, at that moment they were not for Rab.

"I'm gaun tae smash in this hut," was his ultimate recognisable statement. I thought it was time to get going. "Please yersel," I said and hastily left.

I met McCafferty further along the site. "Rab Tunnock is smashing up the hut," I informed him. "Better look out. He's pure mental."

"Don't worry I'll take care o' that nut." He added, "Ye'd better get hame. There's nae point in hingin' aboot on a day like this. I'll put yer time in tae five, but be sure tae be in sharp tomorrow and tell the rest o' the layabouts tae be in sharp as well."

"Sure Harry, we'll a' be in sharp."

"That'll be the day," he jeered.

I walked on shivering. I put my hands in my pockets and passed the apprentice laying brick in slow motion like a phantom in the fog.

"Mind!" McCafferty shouted, "be in sharp!"

"Get stuffed!" I said, but not too loud, and thanked God I wasn't paid off yet.

9

"Did ye hear that McCluskie's oot!" declared my mother when I was just in from work and not in a great mood.

"Who?"

"Ye know fine. Him from along the road. Him that did auld Muncie in."

"Oh him. Whit's for dinner?"

"Ye'll see when it's ready!" she snapped and charged through to the kitchenette, adding, "the trouble wi' you is that you're interested in nothin' but yersel."

"How should I be interested in McCluskie. He's nothin' but a heid-banger."

"He's no' the only one."

"Don't gie me that fork," I instructed when she placed some chips and egg on the table. "It's a' rust."

She studied the fork. "Nothin' wrang wi' it. It must be great tae have servants."

"It must be great tae have cutlery."

"Anyway, I think it's terrible," she said.

"Ye mean this fork?"

"I mean it's terrible that McCluskie's oot."

"I thought ye were pally wi' his auld wife."

"I feel sorry for her right enough havin' a son like that, but I've nae time for him."

"I'm sure he's worried."

"Well, worried or no', I hear folks are gettin' up a petition tae put the McCluskies oot their hoose."

"The trouble wi' folk," I informed her, "is that they should mind their ain business, including yersel."

"Oh sure, everybody should mind their ain business, then we could a' get murdered in oor beds."

"As far as I can remember the verdict was manslaughter."

"It was murder. The poor auld soul had his heid caved in."

"Well, if your heid banged aff the pavement it might cave in. Anyway, shut up. I want tae read the paper."

I propped the paper up against the milk bottle, but I was really thinking fancy McCluskie getting out. I was sure he would have been put away for eight years. In fact I was hoping he would have been put away for eight years. Not that I gave a damn about Muncie.

At one time McCluskie had been my one and only pal — a long time ago — when we were at school. In those days we had very fine ideas about our future. He was going to be a fireman and I was going to be a veterinary surgeon. I liked the sound of that. But things didn't work out. He got a job in the distillery and I got started as an apprentice brickie. There had been nothing sensational about him then. He was a short, beefy, fair-haired lad with the scrubbed look that blond folk have. "A nice boy," was my mother's comment. "I wish you looked half as tidy as him. That hair o' yours is always hingin' ower yer eyes." Our main pastime had been to go to the pictures as often as we could afford it and throw apple stumps at the heads in front of us. In the fine weather we would read dirty magazines whilst sunning ourselves on top of the bin lids. But we became fed up with the pictures and dirty magazines and took to drinking. This was mainly because of McCluskie's easy access to the stuff. On Fridays he would come along for me carrying a lemonade bottle filled with undiluted spirits sneaked from the distillery. We would drink this in an old wash-house, and finish up rolling about the floor and being violently sick more often than not. We stayed out as late as possible so I could stagger to bed undetected while my mother was involved in the television, as she was even in these days. We enjoyed the excitement of this illicit drinking even if we never felt well. My mother would remark on how puky I looked but she was never suspicious. Maybe she thought it was a stage I was going through.

It all came to a head one Friday night when my mother was gossiping outside the close with a neighbour. Being drunker earlier than usual we had misjudged the time. The two of us were hitting off the fence as we rolled along the road. I must have been getting to the chronic stage because I couldn't see very well.

"Stop that stupid carry on," she said abstractedly in the middle of her discussion. McCluskie rolled on by heedlessly but I collapsed over the fence.

"The boy looks right bad," the neighbour said.

"In the name o' God whit's up wi' ye?" said my mother.

"I canny see!" I gasped out, then sank to the pavement.

"Looks like he's got meningitis," said the neighbour.

"Get me a doctor, quick!" I pleaded.

This statement struck a false note with my mother. She pulled my head up by the hair and smelled my breath.

"He's bloody well drunk. 'Phone the doctor, Aggie, an' I'll get him aff the pavement."

I wasn't well for a fortnight. During that time my mother kept up a tirade of abuse between plates of tinned tomato soup. I never knew what happened to McCluskie but for the time being I had had enough of booze. Gradually I came out of my misery and returned to work. I lost touch with him and my mother had altered her opinion.

"I never want tae see that fella near this hoose again," was her command.

In those days she did have some jurisdiction over me, but it was a lonely business going to the pictures on your own or watching the telly with mother. I longed for a bit of excitement. Once or twice I went to the washhouse on a Friday hoping McCluskie would show up even without the lemonade bottle. Once in desperation I went straight from the site to the distillery in the chance I would bump into him. Sure enough I got there in time to see him sauntering along the road with another fella. Happiness surged through me at the sight of his moon face. Great, I thought, I was going to live again. I couldn't reach him quick enough.

"How's it gaun John?" I said.

The laughter faded from his face. "Tolerable son, tolerable," he said coolly. He walked on without as much as a slowdown. My face flushed as if the skin had been stripped off. I had to keep going. I walked straight on, as if I was wound up, right through the distillery gate.

"Where do you think you're goin'? asked the gateman.

"Jist waitin' for somebody," I mumbled.

"Well wait back doon the road."

I hung around for a minute outside the distillery for appearance's sake and to keep me from catching up with McCluskie, then slowly I returned home.

I went through a bad period at that time. I stayed in at nights. Then I would pace up and down staring out of the window wondering if I could risk going out for a walk without folk taking a note of my loneliness. I could have become a recluse without any bother. Finally, one Friday I was adventurous enough to buy a half bottle of cheap wine from the licensed grocer. I drank it in the seclusion of my bedroom. Courage hardened in my nerve cells enough to make me move outwards. I moved along to the first pub I came to, which was the Paxton Arms. Everybody was standing about in casual attitudes talking and laughing, but I was stiff with embarrassment. I knew the lonely sign was written all over me. Desperately I ordered a pint of beer and found it gassy and hard to swallow. A grizzled looking guy came over and stood beside me. His eyes were wise and searching. The heat rose within me.

"Does yer mither know ye're oot?" he asked. I stood rigid and scarlet.

"Relax son. I'm no' gaun tae report ye for bein' under age if the barman canny see that himsel."

"I'm auld enough."

"Sure — auld enough tae drink shandy."

"Look mister," I said, "shut yer face or I'll shut it for ye!"

He laughed. "Ach, ye widny hit an auld man. Here I'll buy ye a decent drink."

He ordered two whiskies and placed one before me, saying solemnly, "My name is Patrick Grant McDonald, but you can call me Paddy."

From then my social life began.

I saw McCluskie once or twice in the Paxton after that, but I looked through him. He didn't bother me. He looked through me. I told Paddy McDonald that McCluskie was in the habit of stealing money from his mother. After that I never saw him in the Paxton again. Maybe Paddy had influence. Anyway I became one of the regulars and forgot about McCluskie. Then last year he hit the headlines. Apparently he was running round with some crazy gang out of the district and he was selling Muncie, the nightwatchman of Paterson's Sawmills, bottles of undiluted whisky. Muncie watered this down and sold the stuff at a nice profit. The gang always drank in his hut before they went out on the rampage. One night a fight broke out. Muncie must have interfered. He finished up with his skull smashed on a paving stone. McCluskie was charged. It could have happened to anyone but I was glad because I figured he had it coming. Now he was out it seemed a bit of an anti-climax. Then I thought why bother about McCluskie. He was nothing to me now one way or another.

At least that was what I thought until I got Big Joe along the road to the site on Monday morning.

"I hear there's gaun tae be a new start," he informed me. That wasn't worth a reply. There were always new starts on a Monday.

"Did ye hear whit I said?" he repeated.

"Aye — so what?"

"I'll tell ye so what. It's McCluskie that's the new start. Him that did auld Muncie in."

"How did he manage that?" I asked. "He's never worked on the sites."

"Well, ye know McCafferty always has a soft spot for jailbirds since his son-in-law did time for ripping copper off an electric cable and putting the lights oot all over oor world. He was a pushover for McCluskie."

"Whit can he dae on the buildin'?" My mind was trying to cope with this set of circumstances.

"Anybody can dae general labourin'. It's better than hard labourin'." He went into convulsions at his joke.

"Ye're no' funny. I don't want tae work beside that murderin' bastard."

"I didny know ye were carryin' a cross for Muncie. I heard he was very fond o' wee lassies."

"In this place everybody gets a name for somethin'," I said angrily.

As I said before I didn't give a damn about Muncie but it had taken me seven years to get over McCluskie. Now I might be back to where I started. I retreated into silence as we pushed on.

Sure enough, when we got into the hut there was McCluskie sitting in the corner. I looked him over furtively. He had changed a lot. He used to be beefy and red-faced. Now he was lean and pale. He gave me no sign of recognition. His eyes were on his feet. The squad were doing the usual Monday morning routine of grumbles about hangovers and giving highly coloured versions of their weekend, and kicking empty cans from Friday afternoon's booze-up. I took no part in this. I was too busy watching McCluskie. He rose to his feet and said, "I'm new at this game fellas," then laughed — a pitiful attempt at a laugh anyway. "I don't know whit I'm supposed tae dae, so if ye could gie me a clue like—"

For a minute nobody said anything. Then Fitty Peters, who is always on the ball, started to sing *Jailer Bring Me Water*.

As everybody is always ready for a laugh, especially on a Monday which is a very nervous day, we all joined in. McCluskie turned pink.

He sat down, scratched his head and joined in as well. Then everybody went silent. He was left singing "My throat is kind of dry" on his own. In an offhand way I noticed that his gear was worse than mine. He had been charged in the summer and still had the open season gear. The thin stylish jacket, the coffee-coloured strides, the suede shoes, topped off with a yellow tee-shirt. All great for the beach but weird on a building site. I didn't feel like laughing any more, but he wasn't going to get any sympathy from me so I hurriedly gathered up my tools and left for the weary load ahead. Some folk had it coming to them and that was all there was to it.

"Is that the fella that murdered auld Muncie?" the apprentice asked me in a reverent tone.

"It wis manslaughter — no' murder."

The apprentice sickened me. He had seen nothing, done nothing and was always a goody.

"Whit's the difference?" he asked.

"Well, the difference is, if I take this brick hammer an' smash it ower yer heid, that would be murder. On the other haun', if I accidently push ye aff the scaffolding when we get up, that's manslaughter."

"Oh," he replied.

"But there's nae point in tellin' ye anything. Ye're too thick."

"I'm learnin'," he said and added quickly, "so if I accidently pushed you aff it wid still be manslaughter."

I gave him a long look. You can never trust anyone. "That wid be a bloody miracle."

Eventually the whistle blew. I was dying for the break, but I wasn't keen to see McCluskie again.

He wasn't in the hut when I came in and I was hopeful he had chucked it. Then he arrived along with McCafferty. Conversation ceased. McCafferty brought out his flask of soup unaware of the silence. McCluskie brought out a paper bag from his pocket and produced a flattened pie. He looked as miserable as hell. Joe Duffy unfolded the newspaper and said straightaway, "Fancy, here's a chap that got eight years for murderin' his wife. Ye'd have thought he wid have got aff. Just shows some folks are lucky and some folks are no'."

McCafferty munched on oblivious to the nudges and winks. He said to McCluskie, "Are ye gettin' the hing o' things noo?"

"I suppose so," answered McCluskie. His eyes were bleak.

"That's the game," said McCafferty. He looked around us trustingly.

"The lads here will show ye the ropes. They're no' a bad lot. That right Fitty?"

Fitty looked in the other direction. "Depends," he said.

"On whit?" said McCafferty. It was beginning to dawn on him that all was not light and happiness.

"Depends if we feel like it," said Big Joe.

McCafferty's face went sour. "Listen you lot. I don't want any trouble. McCluskie has had a bad break."

"So did Muncie, if ye ask me," said Randy Smith.

Suddenly McCluskie arose and stood stiff with fists clenched.

"Ye can stick yer job, Harry. There's a lot better men in the stir than whit's in here, and as for *you*—" I looked up startled to see that he was addressing me. "I can see ye don't want tae know me, though I wis good enough for ye when I wis gettin' ye free drink at one time."

His point of view left me speechless. Then I said, "For years ye widny even say hullo to me, an' as for yer free drink. It wis lethal. Ye nearly killed me wi' it."

"Naw, it wis Muncie he killed," interrupted Fitty. "You were lucky. You got away." There was uproarious laughter.

"Harry," pleaded McCluskie, "pay me aff and let me oot o' here. If ye pay me aff the auld wife will get broo money. Dae us that favour."

McCafferty shrugged. "Away hame and I'll send yer cards on. I'll say ye wereny fit for the buildin'."

McCluskie nodded. He gave us a long stare. Now we looked at our feet. He looked around as if he had forgotten something. There was only his empty paper bag. He crumpled it and put it in the bucket as though he was obliged to leave the place tidy. Then he left.

Somebody said, "That's got rid o' that bugger anyway. He should never have started."

McCafferty said, "Ye canny tell wi' folk. Some are no' cut oot for the buildin'."

"That's true," said Big Joe, "he wis mair suited for a distillery."

"Mind ye," said McCafferty, "I never held Muncie against him."

"Muncie wis nae loss tae onybody," said Fitty Peters. "He deserved it."

I looked out of the hut door. I could still see McCluskie in the distance and I couldn't help thinking we never gave him much of a chance. After all it was only manslaughter not murder, and nobody had given a damn about Muncie anyway.

10

It was Christmas Day, a Saturday. The streets were covered in ice and nothing was moving except me. There was not a soul, a dog or even a bus in sight and worst of all I suspected the pubs would be closed. I headed in the direction of the Paxton with my mother's Christmas message ringing in my ears.

"Where's yer Christmas present ye ask? Well, where's mine? Every year it's the same. Not a sausage dae I get aff ye. No' even an extra pound an' a' the neighbours showin' aff their presents. Well, I'm sick o' it—"

"And a merry Christmas to you!" I had shouted as I walked out.

I stood outside the Paxton. My pessimism was justified. It was shuttered and bare, but there was a drone of voices from somewhere. I went round the back and there was Baldy Patterson and Big Mick swaying over a prone figure on the gravel. Baldy was waving an open bottle of wine about as he studied the object. It was Paddy McDonald. He was blue, but breathing.

"Better get him aff the ice. He'll die o' exposure," I said.

"That's jist whit I wis sayin'," replied Baldy as he splashed me with the wine.

"I'd rather have that doon ma throat," I told him.

He handed me the bottle. It was great how they managed this so early. But when it came to the wine they could always work the miracle.

"How long has he been lyin' here?" I asked.

"Maybe a' night. We jist came alang tae see if the place wis open."

"There's nothin' open the day except the hotels."

"We don't fancy the hotels," said Big Mick.

I wasn't surprised. Unshaven, bloodshot and filthy, they were not exactly the hotel type.

"Anyway," said Baldy, "the Paxton is supposed tae open at twelve."

I took heart at the words but I knew he wouldn't have a clue about anything, even that it was Christmas Day. Paddy twitched in his sleep.

"Whit are ye gaun tae dae aboot him? He'll get pneumonia."

"He's no' ma responsibility," said Big Mick.

"Nor mine," said Baldy, but to prove he had Paddy's welfare at heart he gave him a kick saying, "Get up ya stupid bastard!"

Paddy merely turned on his side. I was dying to get away but it was difficult to leave a potential corpse, especially at this time of the year.

"Can ye no' drag him up tae his hoose?" though I knew this was beyond their capabilities.

"Better leave him for the polis," said Big Mick. "They'll take care o' him."

"The polis will never see him roon' here." I tried to

haul him up but he was as limp as a bundle of rags. They both watched me with indifference.

"Ye're wastin' yer time. When the Paxton opens we'll drag him in an' let Flossie take care o' him."

I let Paddy go and he slithered down the wall. Baldy handed round the bottle and we studied the problem. Mick finished the wine and rolled the bottle along the ground.

"Keep the place tidy," said Baldy. He flung it in the bushes.

Conversation petered out. Sullenly we regarded Paddy. For the sake of doing something I took his pulse. It was faint but flickering. Anyway his breath steamed the air. What bloody luck to walk into this set-up. I leaned against the wall and folded my arms. I was beginning to freeze.

Finally Mick said, "Whit's the time?"

"Time we wir away. Ye might as well face facts. The Paxton is no' gaun tae open the day. It's Christmas."

Baldy was amazed. "Is it?"

"Aye. Good King Wenceslas an' a' that."

"An' whit did ye get frae Santa then?" asked Mick with a bronchial laugh.

"A bottle o' wine," said Baldy promptly, "an' guess who Santa is?"

"Who?" asked Mick.

I said nothing. They were getting on my nerves.

"Paddy here. He wis lyin' on the ground wi' a bottle stickin' oot his pocket for his auld mate."

"Christ, ye'd rob the deid," I said.

"He bloody well looks deid," said Baldy giving Paddy another kick.

"Listen!" said Mick. "There's somebody in there."

We listened. We could hear the noise of dishes being clattered.

"An' look," said Baldy, "the light's on."

Sure enough there was a beam of light from the back window.

We all ran round to the front. The door was still shut. We banged it with our feet. Eventually the door opened and Flossie peered out. His face was all screwed up.

"For God's sake, can ye no' wait?"

"How much longer?" I asked. "Paddy McDonald is lyin' roon' the back an' he looks as if he's gaun tae kick the bucket any minute."

"Well he can kick it ootside. He's no' gaun tae mess up things in here." He slammed the door in our faces.

"That's fuckin' marvellous," said Big Mick.

"Ach, I'm away," said Baldy. "I think I've got a bottle planked somewhere in the Drive."

"For Christ's sake! How did ye no' mention that sooner," said Big Mick.

They stumbled off without a backward glance.

I thought I had better see to Paddy. It was a surprise to find he had managed an upright position. His arms were stretched against the wall as if he was holding it up. He began to thump it.

"Haud on Paddy. It's gaun tae open soon."

He tried to speak, but his teeth just chattered. I led him round to the front.

"Ma feet," he moaned. "I canny feel them."

"Maybe ye've been up in the Yukon an' got the frostbite. C'mon, ye'll be a' right once we get inside. It's gaun tae open soon."

By the time we reached the entrance Flossie was unlocking the door. Paddy tried hard to resurrect himself but Flossie said, "He's no' gettin' in here in that condition."

I pushed past him dragging Paddy along with me, and placed him on a chair.

"Get us two haufs quick, before I have tae call an ambulance."

The word "ambulance" knocked the argument out of Flossie. He served us rapidly.

"Get this hauf doon ye!" I ordered Paddy. He did as he was told then gave a long quiver and relaxed.

"Thanks son," he said.

I didn't like the look of him. His eyelids and lips were purple. I looked around for a bit of distraction but the bar was empty. Doubtless folk would be celebrating in the comfort of their homes with the turkey and plumduff. My mother didn't go in for that sort of thing. Though maybe she would stretch a point when I got back and produce a steak pie and jelly. This effort would be rounded off with a box of five cigars. To hell with Christmas.

Paddy began to fumble in his pocket but he gave it up and fell asleep with his head on the table. I shook him to make sure he was only sleeping. He looked at me with a blind stare. Then the sight returned. He said, "I don't feel sae good. The worst I've ever felt."

The blind stare came on again. He slumped forward. Flossie looked over with suspicion. I straightened Paddy against the chair but he lolled about like a rag doll. I approached the bar. "Right Flossie, get an ambulance."

Flossie was outraged. "Whit dae ye think this is — a surgery?"

"If ye don't get one ye might have tae attend an inquest."

Flossie was convinced. He darted through to the 'phone. I checked with Paddy again. He had gone back to the fumbling stage.

"Whit are ye lookin' for?"

He gestured for me to be quiet. Finally he produced two crumpled pound notes.

"Buy yersel a drink."

The notes were greasy and torn. I pushed them back. "Haud on tae them Paddy."

"Naw, naw. I want ye tae have a drink."

To save any argument I shoved them in my pocket and got two whiskies with my own respectable pound note. Gradually Paddy began to look a bit better. His face was now pallid instead of ashen.

"How long were ye lyin' ootside anyway?"

"I don't know. Maybe since last night."

"Good God man, it's a miracle you're no' deid!"

"I'm a hard man tae kill, but I think —"

Whatever he thought I don't know for his eyes went glassy again.

"Did ye 'phone the ambulance?" I shouted to Flossie. He was talking to a couple of fellas who had just arrived.

"Aye," Flossie hissed over, "but keep yer voice doon. We don't want customers tae think they're in a morgue. We want tae keep the place a bit cheery like."

"Somethin' wrang wi' Paddy?" asked one of the fellas, "or is he jist stoned?"

"Stoned cold is mair like it. Actually he's a sick man."

I said to Flossie, "Maybe ye could show a bit o' Christmas spirit an' gie Paddy a drink before he withdraws his custom."

The fellas nodded in agreement. Flossie looked pained but put two small glasses on the counter. I swallowed mine and placed the other one before Paddy. He tried to lift it to his mouth but it smashed on to the floor. I wished the ambulance would hurry. Then he spoke as if we had just met. "Pleased tae see ye Mac. I thought we had fell oot."

"I widny fall oot wi' you."

"Aye ye did. Mind ye thought I wis a polis informer?" He attempted a laugh. "I widny even inform them the time o' day."

He went quiet again. I could hear the distant whine of an ambulance. Again he came out of his reverie. "I don't want it tae get around, but I hivny been feelin' well lately. Ye see, ma hoose wis burnt doon the other night. A' ma pigeons are deid. Maybe the cat as well."

I looked away in case he was going to cry, but he carried on dry-eyed. "Ye don't happen tae know o' anybody who takes in ludgers. I widny be any bother."

I had to smile. "Afraid not Paddy."

"Of course," he took a deep breath, "I can always go tae the Drive wi' Baldy an' the team. Though they're no' really ma type."

He lost the thread of things and closed his eyes. The ambulance men entered. "Did somebody send for us?"

Paddy heard this. Painfully he stood up and said with a touch of his old wrath. "It wisny for me I hope!"

I nodded to them and jerked my head towards Paddy. Flossie stopped polishing his glasses and looked over, no doubt sensing a commotion, but there was very little for at that point Paddy crashed back on to the floor and lay like a log. An ambulance man knelt down beside him and felt his pulse. He didn't have to say anything. It was plain he was gone. The other one asked me, "Are you a relative?"

"Jist an acquaintance."

"Bloody shame," said a fella at the bar.

"He wisny actually a regular," Flossie explained as though anyone gave a damn, "only a derelict that came in noo an' again —"

"Shut up!" I said.

The ambulance men ignored all this and placed Paddy on a stretcher, then carried him away.

"Did ye know him well?" asked the fella at the bar.

"Well enough."

"Here have a hauf," said the other one.

"No thanks, but thanks all the same, I'm away hame."

"Back already?" asked my mother.

"Aye, everything is deid this morning." This was unintentional.

"By the way, I tried tae get ye somethin' for yer Christmas believe it or no', but everythin' wis shut, so here's two pounds. Buy yersel a present."

Her face went red. "Thanks," she said stiffly, then "I didny mean whit I said earlier on. I know ye didny have much money." She looked at the notes. "They're awfy dirty right enough. Did ye find them?"

"Naw, they're mine. Very legitimate, but I'll take them back if ye don't want them."

She laughed. "I wis only jokin'." Then she kissed me timidly on the cheek.

"Nane o' that stuff," I said. "Away an' get the dinner ready."

She went into the kitchenette. "Happy Christmas!" I called after her. Then I thought of Paddy lying in the morgue, and his burnt-out bothy, his dead pigeons and possibly the cat. I was lucky. I still had five cigars.

11

I suppose it was bound to happen some time. The Arabs say "it is written" and for me it was written.

All the week after Christmas I was in a foul mood. It was a long holiday for the building site worker. My money was gone by Boxing Day. I faced the New Year without a penny in my pocket and Paddy McDonald's death lay heavy like a lump of indigestion. I never went to his funeral or knew of any who did and I never saw the team from the Drive, nor wanted to. Anyway the dead are taken care of. I have my problems.

After being out of circulation for three days I tapped my mother for a pound. This would lessen my chances for a loan at Hogmanay but I had given up caring about the future. With the money I headed for the Paxton and ran into Paddy's hard-boiled nephew, Murdo.

"How's it gaun?" I asked, noting he had a fair bevvy in him. He looked at me with the speculation of the boozer who wonders whether to pick a fight or be friendly. He chose the latter.

"Terrible aboot Paddy," he said.

"Aye," I thought I had better not say too much in case I got the rap for Paddy's death. Murdo's temperament was inclined to blame folk for events. It could be society in general or anybody who was handy. He was a great one for causes and Paddy's would be the latest. Still, I felt bound to add something. "Big funeral wis it?"

"Naebody there except me an' the undertaker."

Quickly I said, "I couldny manage masel. I've been in bed a' week wi' the flu."

He thought over this remark, and accepted it.

"I know ye wid have come if ye could. Paddy wis fond o' ye." He laid his arm, weighing like a ton, on my shoulders.

"Gie that man a double," he said to Flossie. "He's one o' the best."

"Here's tae Paddy, an' wha's like him!" was the toast. Solemnly we clinked our glasses.

"That reminds me," said Flossie, "there's three pound chalked against him on the board. I don't suppose ye want to keep his memory pure an' pay it?"

I admired Flossie's guts, though maybe it was just stupidity.

Murdo glowered. "Of all the mean bastards —"

"That's OK," said Flossie hurriedly, "I wis jist sayin'."

I changed the subject. "Wis there enough money tae bury him then?"

"Oh sure. A man like Paddy doesny need a fancy grave wi' a heidstane. He had as good a coffin as anybody. It wid jist be a wee bit hard tae find the exact spot he wis buried."

"Who wid want tae visit a grave anyway?" I said. "We'll always remember him the way he wis."

"That's true," said Murdo. "Every time I come intae this bar I'll always mind Paddy staunin' at the end o' the counter wi' his glass."

"Always crackin' a joke," I said.

"Aye, always the cheery one."

We stared sadly into space.

"D'ye know," said Murdo breaking the spell, "I'm gaun tae be stony broke this New Year. I've hardly a tosser left whit wi' a' the arrangements. I'm due twenty-five pounds aff the Social Security for Paddy's funeral, but I'll no' lay ma haunds on it for a week or two. You know whit the social is like."

Straightaway I said, "I'm stony masel." There was another silence. "I'll get ye a hauf though," I added in the way of consolation.

Murdo in a bad mood was a grim prospect. He accepted a glass of whisky gratefully. I looked around to see who I could join. Before I could move he said, "Did ye ever consider doin' a job?"

"Whiddy ye mean?" I knew what he meant.

"There's a hoose alang the road jist askin' tae be done. Plenty o' good gear an' maybe money lyin' aboot."

"A hoose? Do ye mean a mansion o' some kind?"

"Naw. It's a tap flat up a close. We could get in through the loft, but I need somebody tae gie me a punt up."

"That's a mug's game. For a start how do we get rid o' the gear?"

"Dead easy. I've got connections."

I wasn't interested. Not that I'm averse to a bit of pauchling. For me the building site was fair game for

102

easy pickings. Many a time I sold Sanny Hamilton, a private contractor, cheap bags of cement and such like. But I didn't fancy house-breaking.

"Mind ye," said Murdo, "I only dae this kind o' thing when I'm stuck. I don't make a livin' at it. But things are gettin' right hard these days. Imagine, nae drink for the New Year."

I agreed. "It hardly stauns thinkin' aboot."

"Well, whit aboot it then?"

"Naw."

His eyes hardened. "Maybe ye're jist yellow."

"Maybe, but if ye come ootside ye'll find oot."

I picked up an empty tumbler. I wasn't going to be unarmed. Murdo always carried a knife. We stared at each other in deadlock.

Finally he said, "Don't get yer back up. It wis only a chance I wis gie'n ye. There's plenty others will take it."

He ordered two pints. I accepted mine without any thanks. Time to get going and leave Murdo to his project. There was no point in getting into a drinking mood. I had about twenty pence in my pocket so I might as well go home. I couldn't even sell anything off the site. Nobody was in business this week. But Murdo's proposition, unacceptable though it was, had set the wheels in motion. How was I going to lay my hands on the ready. There was nothing to pawn in the house except the telly and I might as well go in for armed robbery as attempt that. It would be a sick business scrounging off my mates at the New Year. I would never live it down. Then I began to figure, if Murdo had decided to do a job the house would be robbed anyway. If it wasn't me that got the share it would be somebody else. It would make no difference to the folk in the house, but it would make a difference to my financial standing. I gave Murdo a sidelong glance. He was leaning against the counter, shoulders hunched in the get lost sign. The shutters were down, but I took a chance.

"Anyway," I said as if the subject hadn't been dropped, "these folks might be mates o' mine."

He said coldly, "It's no' likely. The daughter is a Sunday school teacher and her faither is Kilty Cauld Bum McFadjan, the Scottish Nationalist. I don't know aboot the mother, but she must be another bampot. They say she leaves her door open a' the time tae let the cat in and oot."

I was surprised. "Surely no' Cauld Bum! He's no' worth much."

"Don't you believe it. He goes aboot fixing bagpipes. His hoose is stacked oot wi' them. These bagpipes are worth a fortune. Tinker Geordie that plays ootside the Clansman wid gie us at least a fiver for a decent set."

This was different. Kilty Cauld Bum was a joke with most people. Especially us of the socialist class. He cycled about, delivering his pamphlets with his kilt flying in the wind like a bad imitation of Rob Roy. I never had much regard for the highland gentry, but he wasn't even a real one.

"How dae ye know when they'll be oot?"

"Dae ye want a guarantee wi' the job?"

"Forget it then."

"Right."

I noticed his glass was empty. So was mine.

"I might have enough for two half-pints," I said.

"That's more than whit I've got."

I slammed the money on the counter. "Two half-pints Flossie, and chalk the difference up." Flossie complied with tight lips.

Murdo softened. He said, "I know they're oot the night. They're gaun tae a ceilidh up the bay. I know this for a fact because Kilty selt a ticket to one o' ma mates. He said he wid be playin' the bagpipes, an' his wife an' daughter wid be gaun."

There was a pause. "Are ye on then?" asked Murdo.

"I suppose so, but it's only because it's McFadjan. I widny rob any other hoose."

"Don't gie me the sermon. Are ye on or no'?"

"Right."

We shook hands on the matter.

At ten o'clock the same night we were standing on the top floor of a tenement and facing McFadjan's door. We took the precaution of trying it just in case it wasn't locked, but of course it was. We peered through the letter-box, and all was black. We peered through the letter-box of the flat opposite, and all was black, which was an added bit of luck.

"Right," said Murdo, taking out a torch from his pocket. "Gie's a punt up."

"Whit are ye gaun tae dae anyway?" I asked.

"I jist go alang the rafters for a wee while, bash a hole in the ceiling, then in."

I placed my arms on the wall, at the same time stooping a bit.

He managed to get his feet on my shoulders but the weight was terrible. I straightened myself as best as I could manage, to allow him to reach the trapdoor of the loft.

"It's helluva stiff," he said to my dismay.

He banged on it for ages. The sweat was blinding me.

"For God's sake, hurry! I canny take yer weight much longer."

Finally he eased it open and the weight lifted from me. I could hardly take my arms from the wall to straighten myself, but when I did he had disappeared into the loft.

Nervously I paced about peering over the three flights of stairs. I was supposed to bang on the trapdoor if anyone came. It occurred to me I couldn't reach it, so I prayed no one would come. Then I heard footsteps. Skliff, skliff, they came up on the first landing. Skliff, skliff, up to the second landing. Skliff off into a flat I prayed, but they skliffed right on up to the third. Trying to look casual I knocked on McFadjan's door as if I was a legitimate caller. From the corner of my eye I saw a man and woman approaching. At first they didn't see me.

"Don't think I never seen you winkin' tae that piece behind the bar," the woman was saying.

"I wisny winkin'. There was somethin' in ma eye."

He stopped short when he saw me. I knocked again with a show of impatience.

"The McFadjans are no' in. They're away tae a ceilidh," said the woman.

"Oh dear," I said.

"Have I seen you somewhere afore?" asked the man.

Nervously I shuffled. Then there was a crash from above and a muffled roar.

"They must be in Tommy. I hear somethin'," the woman said.

"Maybe he's burst his bagpipes an' blew hissel up," said the man with a laugh and a wink to me.

The woman banged the door and shouted through

the letter-box, "Are ye in?" She looked at me puzzled. "That's funny, they're no' answerin' an' they left the key wi' me tae let the cat in."

"Don't worry," I said, trying to look normal, "if they're in they'll come oot eventually. But there's nae point in yous two hingin' aboot. It's too cauld."

"H'mm," was her doubtful reply.

The man was losing interest, God bless him.

"Get intae the hoose," he said, "an' mind yer ain business." He put his key in the door. Reluctantly his wife turned away. I knocked on McFadjan's door again. As soon as they disappeared I was getting to hell out of it. The woman closed her door slowly, staring at me all the while. Just then a skinny black cat flew up the stairs. Quickly she opened the door. "Tommy!" she shrieked, "there's somethin' funny goin' on. The cat's still oot, an' there's somebody in there, an' they're no' answerin'."

The cat rubbed itself against my leg in ecstasy. I could have kicked it to death.

"And bring McFadjan's key aff the sideboard," she added.

The man came out in a temper. "Whit the hell's up noo?" he shouted.

She snatched the key from his hand and opened McFadjan's door in a flash. I would have ran off, but I was transfixed with indecision. Anyway there might be a chance to bluff it out. If Murdo kept quiet we might still get away with it.

"Follow me," she commanded. "I don't like the look o' things," and marched up the lobby. I daresay she had guts, but I hated them.

The man muttered, "She canny keep her nose oot o' things."

We followed her into the living room. I noticed it was even worse than ours. A tattered three-piece suite, a carpet nowhere near fitting wall to wall and leaving large surrounds of floorboards, plus an ancient piano adorned by stale photographs and tinny candlesticks. Then she investigated the bedroom while we trailed behind her, shouting, "Is onyody there?" At this point she gave a shriek.

My nerves were cracking. "Whit is it?" said the man, "are they a' deid?"

"Look!" she screamed. We looked. A leg was dangling from the ceiling.

"Who's up there?" she demanded. "Answer me!"

At last came the answer, "Fuckin' Kilroy!"

Murdo might be trapped, but I wasn't. I took to my heels and ran.

I didn't have to worry about drink for Hogmanay. That particular night I was in the police cells. So was Murdo, after the law prised him from the beams where he had been jammed. There was no bones broken, otherwise he would have had the comfort of a hospital bed. My mother bailed me out the next morning and we passed New Year's day in silence watching the television. Murdo and I are putting forward the plea that we were drunk and breaking into lofts for a bet. After all, who in their right mind would break into McFadjan's if they were intending robbery? I think this is a good point. Murdo said we will only get a fine at the most and he promised to pay it off Paddy's funeral money from the social, but whatever happens I knew I had it coming. As the Arabs say, "It is written".

12

It wasn't the usual thing for me to be heading over the hills on a frosty morning instead of lying in bed until midday, then afterwards swilling a couple of inches of beer in my glass in the Paxton. It wasn't usual either being unemployed for a month, but this had happened at the beginning of February. Redundancy was the order of the times for the building site worker, who was in as much demand as a pig at a palace.

I decided to take a saunter through the old Douglas Estate. I hadn't set foot in it since my schooldays. The old lodge cottage was gone, only a bit of broken wall remained to mark the garden where we used to pinch hard green apples which gave you the dreaded diarrhoea and the trees were black and gaunt like monuments to the passing of the cottage and my youth. I reached the stable quarters, deserted, but not quite a ruin yet. It had been the last place to be inhabited when the gentry had abandoned it after a fire had burned the big house to the ground. The loyal workers had hung on here, hopeful that the master would rebuild the place to allow them to return to their happy serfdom. He never did. So the workers left for council houses and factory jobs leaving the estate to marauding poachers, lovers and vagabonds like myself.

I studied the many desecrated doors facing me, splintered and barely hanging on by their hinges. Which one was it that another boy and myself had pushed open with great effort to explore its secrets? It had been solid and in good condition then. Steep, wooden stairs had confronted us. The boy had climbed up recklessly, but I had hung back. I remembered having a foreboding about those stairs.

"C'mon fearty," the boy had shouted.

"I canny." I couldn't explain, but my legs were paralysed when I placed them on the stairs.

"It's great up here. There's furniture an' every-thin'."

I had forced myself up, fighting against an invisible weight pressing on me. When I reached the top I had been blinded by the sun shining through the skylight. Except for the boy's gaping grin I couldn't see anything clearly other than a vague impression of rafters above me and a bed in the corner.

"This is a great wee den," the boy had said. "We could play here every day and naebody wid know."

He was full of enthusiasm and probably right. But all I could feel was iciness — a dreadful iciness on that warm summer day. My teeth had chattered.

"It's c-cauld in here," I had mumbled.

"Cauld! Ye must be jokin'."

I hadn't waited. I rushed down the stairs ignoring the boy's taunts.

We had returned home together without saying much and he never played with me again. Maybe that's why I don't remember his name. I never found out what had created that icy sensation and I never heard of any sinister tale about the stables. Maybe I just imagined it.

Now I wondered where the door was. I kicked the one facing me wide open but there were no stairs, just a tangled mass of rubble and felt only the normal iciness of a February day without any past impression. I also felt cheated, because then it had all been so important. We scruffy kids had been so worthless compared to the grandeur of the nobleman's wonderland. Even after he had gone the "Trespassers Will Be Prosecuted" notice had remained to warn us not to enjoy what once had been his. But now the bluff was called. The estate was finished. Even the bushes intruding over the estate road in order to establish their position were wasting their effort. It was down on the redevelopment plan that in one year's time everything would be levelled to the ground in order to build a school for the increasing number of undisciplined and unappreciative council house kids.

A few yards onwards I came across the "hut wi' the hooks" as we called it, reduced to a pile of black rotting planks of wood. Once the hut had been used to hang game or venison until it was decayed enough to eat but when we took it over it was merely used as a base for hide and seek or whatever. At the worst it was a good shelter. Yet I was never too sure of it except when there was a gang of us around. When you were alone and looked at it back over your shoulder as you were leaving you got this funny feeling. At least I did. I remember sitting on its wooden steps with a black dog for company — one of those nameless animals that walked with anyone at all when it took the notion. The dog had shivered, whined and raised the hairs on its back. For me that was proof that the place was haunted. Of course condemning places as being haunted was a vocation with the kids in my day. It ranged from the outgoing community centre to Faroni's chip shop if you had to pass them in the dark and they were closed. Even your own back green wasn't above suspicion if you were ordered to bring in a shirt from the line in the dark and it was stiff with frost waiting for you with outstretched arms. Wee Peter Ratchitt swore blind that he had peered in through our classroom window at ten o'clock one night and saw the ghost of a long dead janitor cleaning the other side of the pane. He was a notorious liar, wee Peter, but on that subject we believed him. We had "being haunted" on the brain.

One late summer evening twelve years ago I had sat on the steps of this hut with two pals. We were tired out playing cowboys and Indians or Tarzan or corpses hanging from the hooks. Strewn all around us were trampled bushes and bits of branches, so we sat in brooding silence for a while scratching our midge bites. Then it began to dawn on us it was dark. Everything looked different. Bushes and trees were assuming the shapes of hunchbacks and Draculas. One of the pals, Bobby Smith, said, "It's in a place like this ye see Frankenstein crashing through the trees."

We peered about us and had to admit by the look of things any kind of weird character could show up.

"I think I'll go hame," said the other pal. "My ma will kill me for bein' oot sae late."

"So will mine," I said.

"Couple o' cowardy custards," said Bobby Smith.

"I'm no' a coward!" I shouted.

"Ye are so! Ye're feart o' yer mother, an' ye're feart o' this place in the dark."

I was stung into a show of bravado. "I'll prove I'm no' as feart as yous two."

"How?" asked Smith.

I tried to think of something impressive. Then I got an idea that would let me head home at the same time.

"I'll go a hundred paces in front. Then I'll wait for the two o' ye at the lodge."

"Ye mean ye'll walk through this place yersel!" said the other one in a tone of awe.

"Aye." Inwardly I was aghast at the prospect. But it was too late now. I had flung down the gauntlet.

Smith said, "I'll bet ye'll no' dae it."

"Whit are ye bettin'?"

This was a difficult question. We didn't own much. Smith searched about his pockets and brought out a pocket-knife.

"This is one o' the sharpest knives ye can get. I'll bet this against yon cricket bat ye were playin' wi' yesterday."

He flicked the knife open. I couldn't see its qualifications in the dusk. Anyway I didn't care how sharp it was. I didn't care about the cricket bat. I had found it in the council dump and I could get another one any time. What bothered me was the journey down to the lodge. I stared into the grey void ahead and said, "Right then, start counting up to a hundred, an' follow."

Without a backward glance I began running down the estate road looking neither to the right or left lest I spied some horrific creature waiting for me. I could hear Smith's voice counting, "Forty-eight, Forty-nine—", while I kept running until I could no longer hear him, at the same time willing my brain to remain blank from the memory of some awful scene from a film that might creep in. Then an idea occurred which almost made me forget my terror. I almost wet myself thinking about it. It was this. I would hide behind a tree near the road and when the other two passed I would give out loud panting noises or even mad fiendish laughter terrifying them out of their wits. Then I would take a short-cut through the woods to the lodge and be there in bags of time before them. I scrambled up the grassy verge and took up my post behind a tree. Even in the dusk I had a good view of the road — so I waited. I waited and waited but they didn't come. I became colder and colder as the panic rose again. Something must have happened to them. I figured whatever it was could happen to me so I'd better get back to that lodge pronto.

I didn't even try to find the short-cut. Blindly I waded through tall weeds and bumped into trees. Then I plunged into a bog camouflaged with thistledown. Keep going I told myself. I must come out somewhere and I did. One second I was squelching through bog and the next I was hurtling downwards. I rolled over bits of wire, broken bottles and bundles of smelly stuff, and just managed to grab on to a thick bush to stop myself landing at the bottom of this pit, which I recalled was an illegal rubbish dump. With difficulty but determination I scrambled upwards, bruised, bleeding and stinking horribly. When I finally crawled into the house my mother went mad at the sight of me. She only refrained from battering me because of the blood dripping over the linoleum. I was ordered to divest myself of all clothing while she bathed my cuts nagging at me all the time, but I was comforted if humiliated, for God knows what had happened to the other two. Next day I was sent to school as usual. Even if my face and legs were a mass of criss-cross cuts I could still walk and that was good enough for my mother. There were no sensational developments because the other two were in the playground as large as life.

"Whit happened tae ye last night?" I asked Smith's companion. "I waited at the lodge for ages."

"We didny come doon the estate road. Smith knew a short-cut ower the wall on tae the main road."

He stared into my face. "Whit happened tae you?"

"Mind yer ain business, ya cheatin' wee coward."

The bell cut short any further discussions. I made a beeline for Smith at playtime. He let forth loud guffaws of laughter at the sight of me, but he didn't laugh long. I knocked him to the ground and pummelled into him.

"Where's ma knife?" I said as I kicked him.

Blubbering like a first-class infant he gabbled, "Leave me alone an ye'll get it."

So for a day I was a hero and kept Smith's knife in a drawer for a long time as a souvenir. It was no use for anything else for it could hardly cut paper. Eventually my mother threw it in the bin.

Yes, these were the days of real adventure, real heroes and real villains. Now it was all grind, booze or trying to get by on the dole.

The damp, cold air cut through my reveries and I decided it was time to get going. As a gesture I patted the clammy wet wood of the remains of the hut a farewell. It had been once a refuge to the ghost seekers and at heart I was still one. Any old ghost would have pleased me. Even the faintest suggestion of one. Anything, just anything to give me a hint of something beyond.

Quickly I walked back through the estate where the trees were still hopeful and came over the hill. I passed a heap of charred ash and blackened stone which had been Paddy McDonald's home. Scattered around this debacle was an ancient cooker, a bit of table and a half-burned sofa, the same one that I had sat on along with Paddy's cat. It would be something to see that cat sitting there right now. It would give a bit of justification to everything. You could think then, if you were that way inclined, that Paddy's spirit was inside the cat. But the fact was that there was no cat, no spirit, and not even a bit of singed fur. To hell with it all; I would make my own ghost. I picked up a piece of blackened char and marked on a bit of wall that remained "PADDY WILL RETURN" then left quickly before anyone saw me.

13

The queue at the unemployment exchange had slowed down to a standstill.

"Whit's the hold-up?" asked the wee fellow in front of me.

"Sounds as if somebody's no' pleased."

"Who wid be in this place an' nae work."

"Ye'd be surprised," said another, "work wid kill some folk."

I suspected he was referring to Big Mick sprawled comfortably along the bench behind us, swigging a bottle of wine.

"Are ye lookin' for a job?" I asked him.

"Naw — jist waitin' on Baldy."

"Great innit," said the wee fella. "All the home comforts. Drink while you wait."

"An' why no'?" said Mick. "There's nae law against it. Here, d'ye want a gargle?" He offered me the bottle. To be sociable I took a mouthful.

"Ye're no' frightened," said the wee fella, "ye could get typhoid drinkin' efter him."

"Who's worryin'. Ye could get it anyway. The

niggers tramp doon the grapes for the wine wi' their feet," I said.

I suspected the wee fella was peeved because he hadn't been offered any.

Somebody said, "I mind ma faither tellin' me that in his day ye wereny allowed tae smoke in the Broo, never mind drink."

"That wis in the dark ages afore Keir Hardie."

"Never heard o' him. Here, whit's the racket aboot?"

"Ye might guess. It's Baldy Patterson."

We stopped talking to hear all the better.

"You've already had your money sent out," the clerk was saying.

"Indeed and I have not!" replied Baldy with heat. "Big Mick back there will tell you." He shouted, "That right Mick?"

"Aye, that's the God's truth," Mick shouted back waving his bottle about.

"Are you here on business?" asked the clerk.

"Naw, I'm jist waitin' on Baldy."

"Then wait outside."

Big Mick leaned back all the more complacently and took another swig from the bottle.

"Where did ye say ye sent it?" Baldy was asking. "Ye know I've got nae fixed address." He made this sound like a reference.

"I'm aware of that," the clerk replied with an exasperated sigh. "I sent it where I always send it, care of William Brown, twelve Mid Street. I suggest you make your enquiries there."

I remembered the situation. Billy now had a legitimate address. He had moved from the derelict Drive to the slightly less derelict Mid Street through a lucky break. His uncle had died and Billy fell heir to his room and kitchen.

"So," the clerk continued, "the matter is out of our hands, and if you are looking for work I'm afraid there is nothing."

"Work ma arse!" said Baldy, "I'm lookin' for money."

"Next please," said the clerk.

The wee fella pushed Baldy aside and took the position over.

"Anythin' in the scaffoldin' line?"

"Nothing," said the clerk, picking up a pad and pencil.

The wee fella persisted. "Can ye no' gie me a card for Cumlocktown then? There might be work there."

"There is nothing there. We have enquired," said the clerk writing on the pad to show he had better things to do.

"Too bad," I said to the wee fella as he turned away. I knew it would be the same for me.

"Bloody hopeless," he said. "I'm thinkin' o' gaun up tae the oil rigs."

"Don't fancy it."

"Well it's the money —"

"Next please!" said the clerk loudly.

"Be seein' ye," I mumbled.

"Anything for brickies?" I enquired. This request was a matter of formality. There had been nothing for the past six weeks.

"Nothing," was the reply.

"Whit aboot labourin' then? Any kind o' labourin' on the sites?"

"Nothing."

On an impulse I asked, though I had no notion of it,

"Whit aboot up north near the oil rigs? Is there nae buildin' gaun on up there?"

He looked at me irritated. It was clear he did not wish any deviation from the word "nothing". "I'm afraid you will have to enquire about that yourself." He began to write on his pad again.

I walked away in time to see an empty wine bottle hurtle through the door. It was in keeping with my sentiments exactly.

I caught up with the wee fella.

"Nothin' doin'?" he asked.

"Nothin'."

"Ye're daft. Go up north. That's where the work an' money is."

"I don't fancy it."

I didn't know why. There wasn't much to stay for. I couldn't think of anybody who would give a damn whether I left or not. I often felt my mother was relieved when I went out. Anyway I knew I irritated her more than usual hanging around the house. I had even lost the guts to complain about the meals or kid her on about anything.

"I'll gie ye the name o' a firm up north that's desperate for brickies," said the wee fella. "Try it."

"I might at that."

Back home I thought I had better mention the subject to my mother — although we had been silent for so long it was difficult to begin.

"Have ye got a cuppa tea ready?" I began, more for the sake of testing out my voice.

"Tea?" she said, as though she had never heard of it.

"Aye, ye know. These wee leaves ye pit in a teapot."

"Put it on yersel," she said.

"Dae ye want one?" I asked, ignoring her coolness.

"Whit's the snag? Ye might as well know I canny lend ye anythin'."

I clenched my teeth. I could get nowhere with this woman.

"I'm no' wantin' the lend o' anythin'." I made the tea and poured her cup out with a grudge.

"Whit I was wonderin'," I said as I handed it to her, "was if I should go up north tae look for work. It's hopeless here."

She was startled. "An' leave me here masel!"

That surprised me. I never considered myself great company for her.

"I wid send ye money."

"I wisny thinkin' aboot the money."

She stared at her cup and blinked her eyes. I could hardly credit there were tears in them. I hoped not. Now that I was talking myself into leaving I was going to be resentful of any opposition.

"Whit aboot yer pals?" she asked, "an' Mrs Smith doonstairs thinks ye're an awfy nice big fella."

"Whit's that got tae dae wi' it?"

"Nothin'," she said, "but ye might no' like it away from hame."

I didn't like to point out that "hame" for me was only a place to sleep and eat. "Besides I can always get other pals," I said.

"Whit aboot Paddy McDonald? He'll miss ye."

Patiently I explained, "Paddy is deid. Dae ye no' remember?"

"Oh aye," she said absently. "Well it's up tae you."

She disappeared into the kitchenette. Apparently she didn't want to discuss it. Next thing she was back.

"Here's a lend o' a pound until ye get yer broo money."

I didn't particularly want it, but I just said "Thanks" and walked out.

I didn't go to the pub. I walked along by the river. Under the bridge in the usual place sat Baldy and Big Mick. There it was, all set out, my future. The wine bottle bulged in Mick's pocket.

"Where are ye gaun?" he asked.

"Naewhere."

He pulled the bottle out and handed it to me. I took a mouthful.

"Did ye get yer money then?" I asked Baldy handing the bottle over to him.

"Aye, Billy found it on a shelf. He wis that drunk this mornin' he forgot it had came — stupid wee sod!"

"Still no' workin'?" asked Mick.

"Naw. Have ye no' heard? There's a depression on."

He laughed. "It's no' affectin' us." Then he became serious. "I know times are bad. Dae ye want a len' o' a fiver?"

I could have laughed myself. I was better off than they would ever be. I was on the point of refusing, then it struck me a fiver would come in handy. Come to think of it, it was necessary.

"Thanks Baldy. I'll pay ye back when I get ma broo money."

He brought out crumpled notes rolled into a ball. It was two fivers. He separated one and handed it to me in the manner of a true philanthropist.

"Tae think," said Mick, "that the bastard has been drinkin' ma money a' mornin'."

"Keep yer hair on. I've got a fiver for us tae spend

the night an' still one left for the morra when the boy here gets his broo money."

Mick looked sheepish. "I wis only jokin'. Sit doon on that plastic mac an' I'll gie ye a dram."

They thought I had nothing and they were bending backwards to give me what they could.

"Whisky?" I asked hopefully.

"Naw, wine. A wee dram o' the wine."

I sat down beside them on the stone. I might as well join them. It was the least I could do. They handed me the bottle while Mick rolled a fag. He studied it to make sure it was a good one then handed it to me with a flourish. I had the feeling I was being initiated. Maybe I could do worse than join them, because at least they had the communal outlook. The booze was usually shared. You might lack comfort but not company. You might be an outcast but you were free. It was tempting.

"Too bad Paddy's no' here," I said.

"Aye." They were suitably silent for a minute but I sensed they were not too concerned. Folk come, folk go. It could be their turn any time. After another swallow I felt talkative. "I wis thinkin' o' gaun up north," I told them. I knew they wouldn't take the statement seriously.

"Whit for?"

"Work."

"Work never done onyone ony good," said Baldy spitting in contempt. "That's for mugs. Look at us, we can drink withoot workin' for it, an' plenty tae eat. A fish supper noo an' again, breid, cheese or a tin o' soup. Eatin' is a fallacy onyway. We're perfectly healthy."

They could have fooled me, but I nodded in agreement.

"So long as ye've enough tae drink, that's the main thing," said Mick wisely. "Onyway, folk up north are no' like us. Especially in the north-east where the work is. You could be dyin' in the street and they wid walk ower ye."

"They don't care," confirmed Baldy. "They widny gie ye a match tae light yer fag."

"Ye've been up north then?" I asked.

"Naw," said Mick, "but I've got a brither that has. He couldny get back here quick enough. They're as mean as fuck."

"I think it's the weather that does it," said Baldy. "They don't get the rain the same as us, but there's an icy wind blawin' a' the time that wid shrivel yer balls."

"If ye had ony," Mick interrupted.

"And that's whit makes them sae mean an' dour. Forget it son. Stay wi' yer ain kind. They're aye the best. That right Mick?"

"It's the very truth."

Maybe they were right. You could say Mick and Baldy were the true gentlemen of the west. Generous, treacherous, vicious and kindly with no admiration for the rich and successful. Yet the difference between them and me was that I liked working. My body was used to it. I preferred to earn my drink and hand in a few pounds to my mother. Their philosophy was all right for them, but not for me, not yet.

"Ye're very likely right," I said.

I decided it was time to go and leave them while there was still some wine in the bottle. They had given me enough.

"I'll have tae get back hame. Ma mother will have the dinner ready."

They looked sad as I arose from the stone. "Cheerio son, be seein' ye."

"Come roon tae the Drive later," Baldy shouted after me. "We'll gie ye a good drink."

"I might at that. Keep a place warm for me."

As I gave them a last glance I wondered if I would ever see them again.

"Have ye got a case or a bag o' some kind?" I asked my mother. "I've made up ma mind. I'm gaun up north tomorrow."

She looked confused and rubbed her cheek. "Dae ye think ye should?"

"I'll have tae gie it a try. This hingin' aboot the hoose is nae use. I'll end up doin' somethin' stupid." I thought I'd better lay it on a bit. "Look how I got intae bother at Hogmanay. Ye know how it is. When ye've nothin' tae dae ye get intae trouble, even if ye're no' lookin' for it. Ye widny like that."

She became indignant. "I got a right showin' up that time the polis came tae the door, an' then yer name in the paper and everythin'. I didny go oot for a week."

"Well, if I'm aff much longer it might get intae the News of the World. It's better that I go an' get work somewhere."

"I suppose so," she conceded. "I'll see if Mrs Smith has somethin' tae put yer clathes in. But how will ye manage the fare? I've hardly any money."

"Jist lend me two pounds and ye can keep the broo money."

She brightened and said, "That's too much."

I waved this aside. "I'll manage. As soon as I get a wage I'll send ye somethin'. An' when I make the big money I'll send ye enough tae get a coloured telly."

Her eyes moistened. To prevent any sentiment I said, "Hurry up wi' the dinner, I'm starvin'."

Afterwards I went to my room to collect my gear. It wasn't impressive. Surprising how little you own when you are faced with the total sum. I wouldn't even have got a balloon from Duds the ragman for the lot. I packed a pullover, two tee-shirts, a pair of pants, two pair of socks, a pair of denims and a pair of boots into Mrs Smith's shabby holdall, and was all set. I looked at my watch. It was only six o'clock. The pubs would be open. A tempting thought to get a couple of pints, but I decided against it, because I might blow the lot and that would be easy. Tonight I would keep my mother company with the telly viewing and please her for once. I counted my notes. Eight in all. Hardly a fortune but folk had set out with less — and starved to death.

I was up early next morning and made myself a cup of tea. No sense in wakening my mother any sooner than necessary. Everything was ready all too quickly. I hung around a bit playing for time. Then I went into her room. She sat up wide awake. "Ye should have got me up," she accused, "I would have made ye somethin' tae eat."

"That's OK. I've had somethin'."

She faced me in her dowdy petticoat, or whatever it's called. She was shaking and seemed to be searching for words. "I'll miss you," was all she said.

"I'll miss you as well." It was the truth. Right then I felt I would genuinely miss her. After all we had been together for twenty-two years. I put my arm round her cold shoulder, "Don't worry, I'll be OK."

I kissed her then left before it got any worse. She knocked on the window as I passed. God, what now.

She opened the window, "Mind and write."

"I will," I assured her. I didn't look back but I knew she would stay there watching until I was out of sight.

As I headed for the bus-stop I began to feel better. It was a bright cold morning with a hint of spring in the air, just enough to make me feel optimistic — and even happy. As I waited at the stop I could pick out the landmarks of my life. Facing me — the Paxton Arms. On the hill behind — the building site. Over the river in front — the derelict Drive. Behind the Drive — the cemetery wherein lay the nameless grave of Paddy McDonald. But that was all finished. It was, goodbye everybody. I was on my way to better things. I was on my way to adventure.

Postscript by Alasdair Gray to Agnes Owen's *Gentlemen of the West*

You will not have read as far as this unless you enjoyed the foregoing tale, so you are probably relieved that Mac has had the sense and energy to step out of the trap his world had become, and leave us with a convincingly hopeful end. This may be the place for someone who has read the novel more than once to explain why he values it, and I will approach my explanation through some remarks about other writing. Readers who dislike windy summaries should read only the last three paragraphs.

There are many reasons why there are few good fictions about folk with low incomes. Great poverty is so disgusting that even the poor hate to be reminded of it, and modest incomes which allow some spare-time pleasure and independence — the incomes which Burns called "honest poverty" — are usually earned by work which feels like slavery. It is a horribly ordinary truth that our imaginations reject most of the living we do, so from the earliest days of recorded wealth we have lifted up our eyes to the wealthy. Wealth is enchanting, even at a distance. It bestows freedom, or a convincing illusion of it. Love, friendship, loss and pain are the materials of every life, but the rich wear their materials with distinction.

Lord Marchmain can choose to die in a Queen Anne four-poster set up in the Chinese drawing-room by the estate carpenters. Getting and spending has not laid waste *his* powers. Which is why (says D. H. Lawrence in his study of Thomas Hardy) artists have an inborn taste for aristocrats. Other classes exist by making things and making money, but unearned wealth allows people to make *themselves*, to develop their distinct individualities. This is what every flower that grows does, and what we all ought to do, says D. H. Lawrence. Maybe Lawrence was influenced by his marriage to the daughter of a German baron, but he was also pointing to a fact. Not just writers but the mass of the public like to imagine they are Gods, owners of great lands and houses, highly paid man-killers, monarchs, priests, politicians and gifted youngsters Making It to the Top. This cast list contains the main characters in fairy stories, the Old Testament, Homer, Shakespeare, all history books until recently, and most of today's newspapers.

But heroes and heroines need servants to help them, buffoons to amuse them, criminals and rabbles to bring out, by contrast, their distinct individualities. Folk with low incomes are not wholly excluded from history and the daily news, and in nearly all the world's great fictions—yes, even in that Homer who most celebrates the courage and cunning of the mighty—a truculent commonsense voice declares that heroic grandeur is not worth the cost of its upkeep, that all but some selfish winners are degraded by it. And a Shakespearian prince tells a band of artists the aim of their profession in language which must have inspired Brecht. "Your job," he says, "is to hold, as 'twere, the mirror up to nature;

to show virtue her own feature, scorn her own image, and the very age and body of the time his form and pressure." The nature mentioned here is human nature, of course, with whatever in land and climate influences it; but to show the whole age and body of a time *to* a time—to reflect the constitution and abuses of a whole commonwealth—is an enormous undertaking. Langland, Chaucer and Sir David Lindsay tackled it. Shakespeare partly tackled it in the history plays. His princes of the church and state, rustic squires and horde of normally unemployable ruffians are drawn into social union by an imperial plundering raid on France. Fluellen and the Archbishop of Canterbury, Prince Hal and Falstaff are of equal dramatic and historical weight. That war needed all of them.

But not until the nineteenth century did a lot of geniuses deliberately describe, with an attempt at equal sympathy, most of the sorts of people who made their nations: Scott first, then at least twelve others in France, England, Russia and America. The French and industrial revolutions had shown that history was what everyone did. A Clydeside engineer, a Corsican corporal, a club of Marseilles republicans, the Lancashire stocking-weavers had changed the world faster than any king or house of lords. In Britain *shake-up* would have been a better word than revolution. None of the mighty had been brought low, but it was now possible to sell books without flattering the aristocracy. It had been joined by whole classes of newly prosperous people with intense curiosity about how wealth and status were acquired and how the less lucky were living. The less lucky had also become literate. Of the three best

English authors after 1850 one had been a child-labourer in a blacking factory, one the kept woman of a London editor, one had earned money as a fiddler in country pubs. Through journalism, translating and a builder's drawing-office they had become popular novelists. They were qualified to show the struggles by which self-respect and money were gained, or barely kept, or wholly lost. While Karl Marx in the British Museum investigated the matter statistically, Dickens, George Eliot and Hardy described dependencies between makers of wealth in workshop, colony and farm, and users of it in the bit of society which called itself Society.

In 1895 *Jude the Obscure* was published. The critics condemned it, and Hardy decided to devote himself to poetry. After that, with few exceptions, there were no writers with the talent and experience to create lowly paid people with considerable viewpoints. Lawrence is the great exception, but in the twenties he deliberately "washed his hands of England". In the mining town where he grew up he had known a community: people who accepted each other for what they had in common as workmates, neighbours, chapel-goers. His mother wanted her children *not* to be common, but professional and moneyed. By his talents he became these things, and found that the professional, talented, wealthy folk he now mixed with, though good friends who recognized his uniqueness, had no community beyond cliques based on love-affairs and conversations about art and ideas. So he went searching through Australia, New Mexico and Italy for a working community like the Eastwood of his childhood, but not based on wage-slavery, and with room for a free spirit like his own.

He left behind a literature almost completely class-bound, and bound to the propertied classes. Galsworthy, Forster, Virginia Woolf, Wyndham Lewis, Aldous Huxley, Elizabeth Bowen are dissimilar writers, yet all describe people so detached from their source of wealth in land, trade or industry that they can ignore it, because it is handled by their bankers. The sensitive among them think this unjust. Forster's Miss Schlegels feel that they stand on an island of golden coins in a wide ocean. Their finely tuned existence consumes the coins, but the sea-waves keep casting more at their feet. The ocean is *people*. The hydraulic pressure which howks the money up from the human depths and casts it on the lucky island is depicted in *The Ragged-Trousered Philanthropists* and *A Scots Quair*, exceptional novels which show the pressures being resisted by working men's defiance and organization. In other fiction, highbrow or popular, the lowly paid have become what they were in Homer's fictions: servants, helpful or truculent eccentrics, a rabble jostling in the street. When authors attempt a larger view of them the usual angle of vision presents something like beetles crawling on each other at the bottom of a tank. There is no suggestion that such people can initiate anything of value, or *be* much, even to themselves.

When I spoke of people looking like beetles crawling in a tank I was not thinking of Greenwood's *Love on the Dole* but of a shallower book called *No Mean City* set in depression Glasgow. Then the image reminded me of some stage plays by Pinter, Orton and Bond. Why did the war with Hitler not change Britain's literary sense of itself? "The only good government" (says Gulley Jimson in *The*

Horse's Mouth) "is a bad government in a fright."
Perhaps. The National Coalition which saw Britain
through the war was a right-wing body, but it would
have been destroyed if it had not mobilized the
nation. It froze profits, took control of industry,
imposed rationing, fixed wages and prices. It got the
unions on its side and ensured that nobody starved
or was unduly exploited. It had spokesmen who said
the post-war Britain would *not* return to the poverty
and unemployment of the inter-war years. To
some extent that promise was honoured. Attlee's
government set up a welfare state. Macmillan's
government did not propose to dismantle it. Butler
enlarged the education grants, and in 1954 Somerset
Maugham was regretting, C. P. Snow applauding,
what they agreed was the first literary fruit of the
newly educated proletariat: *Lucky Jim* by Kingsley
Amis. Then came *Room at the Top* by Braine, *Look
Back in Anger* by Osborne, and reviewers said that a
social revolution had discovered its voice. Yet these
authors had depicted no working-class experiences
whatsoever! Jim Dixon's bumbling irreverence
toward authority is not different in kind from Bertie
Wooster's. Jimmy Porter's contempt for Britain
where "all the good old causes have been won" (he
means full employment and some welfare services)
was voiced at that time by many aristocratic people,
frequently in the press. Joe Lampton thoroughly
enjoyed the lives of the affluent who accepted him.
The most working-class thing about these men is the
sound of their names. They and their authors are
examples of a very commonplace shake-up. Like
Lawrence they entered an affluent part of England
through the educational system. Unlike Lawrence

they enjoyed it and stayed. Nor, in getting there, did they feel they left anything worthwhile behind. Their reputation as messengers of social change came from a temporary failure of nerve by a rich conservative (Maugham) followed by a rich socialist's premature faith that a just nation had at last been founded (Snow). Not the book but the critics showed the state of society, but nobody noticed this.

The first post-war stories to make good use of low-income experience came out of the English north in the sixties and are firmly set there, but tell truths about the whole country. *This Sporting Life* shows a gifted youngster Making It to the Top, and also a love-affair. The hero's talent is rugby football. The machinations by which he pushes his career estrange him from the woman he loves, but as a well-paid sportsman he tries at the end to reclaim her: he has so much to offer! Himself, money, etc. He stands in the street before a burdened aging woman with a shopping bag, and pursues her home, and cannot get her to see him, hear him or acknowledge his existence. He has become that part of the nation which is no use to her. If she were to submit to him and become his mistress or wife it could only be as his property, his appendage. She would feel, look and *be* out of place. If we seek the flaw which cracks the couple apart we can point, if we like, to his ambition, but the flaw is in *Britain*. The comic novel *Billy Liar* is equally desperate. Billy's mother thinks of her family as "just ordinary people". His father says, "I may be just an uneducated working man, but . . ." They take wage-slavery as a norm, and treat their son's imagination as a disease: which it is, even to him, because all he makes with it are fantasies and comic dialogue. He is part of a community which wants to keep him. His boss is so disconcerted by the thought of Billy trying to be a script-writer in London that he refuses to accept his resignation. And at the end Billy skulks away from the London train and the adventurous girl who shared his daydreams. He returns to his parents' council house, cheered by an imaginary army marching at his heels. His imagination will be used not to free but to keep him as he is. Billy loses his lover by crushing his imagination in order to stay in the community. The rugby star loses his lover by developing the skill which takes him out of it. In *Kes* the picture is yet harsher. A victimized schoolboy learns a falconer's skills by nursing a wounded hawk — he is healing his own spirit and teaching it to soar. The community barely tolerates this, and his working brother kills the hawk out of spite. And in *The Loneliness of the Long Distance Runner* the talented sportsman deliberately loses the race, to stop his victory being used by a highly paid headmaster to glorify a kind of boys' prison.

These stories demonstrate the Great British assumption, which is also the Great British lie, that any special talent, initiative or knowledge not advertised as *popular* is a property of the affluent, a luxury of the posh. This particular lie is the unwritten British constitution. It lets Royalty, the government and most professional people raise their wages and keep themselves employed without drawing much attention, and ensures that coalminers who try to do the same are treated like greedy unpatriotic scoundrels and enemies of the state. When a lie is acted upon by most of the highly and lowly paid parts of a nation it must be treated as a fact. Unluckily for the

136

truth, therefore, stories which show how the lie works
can be read as mere matters of fact. Many kindly
conservatives who enjoyed the books I mention
above will have thought: "Yes, that is how they must
live down there. How sad!" The moral then drawn is
not that the nation's wealth should be used to create
productive jobs with high wages and pleasant conditions for everyone, but that talented people of lowly
birth should have easier admission to the society of
those who can make use of them.

It's a pity that storytellers cannot be moralists.
They may invent people who pass moral judgements,
when these are convincing and appropriate, but if
they make their inventions the text of a sermon then
a sermon is all they will write, no matter how well
they have reflected their time. Readers must be
enticed to their own conclusions, which cannot be
predicted. In his study of the novel in the west of
Scotland, Douglas Gifford notes that the commonest
theme is the crushing of imagination by poverty, and
that Archie Hind and I have both written stories
about artists of lowly paid origin who, after tough
struggles, despair of producing anything good.
Douglas regrets that neither novel indicates what he,
a lecturer and critic, lives by indicating: these books
are in a Scottish tradition which has made several
good things. But we were trying to write tragedies
about makers whose work is not wanted by their own
kind. A sense of elevated tradition would only give
them hope of being "taken up" by people of a
different kind.

But perhaps all parables of the talent are fun-
damentally ambiguous. A talent is a measure of silver
as well as an inborn capacity or well-learned skill,

and when we sit down to write what *we* want to read and which nobody else has written, we enjoy a rich privilege. At that moment we are self-employed and self-sufficient. Nothing need dominate us but our sense of the good, exciting or true. Then we put words on paper, notice these are not very good or exciting or true, and the work begins. But what keeps us writing is an occasional heady feeling of being above the world, above everything but a dim, supportive excitement. Wordsworth thought this sense of freedom, power and possibility was an intimation of immortality. It is well known to children whose growth is not pressed down by labour and responsibility; and stories which revive the sense in adults are likely to be read. Working-class novelists usually incarnate it in someone like themselves who has left or will leave his community, or is suffering because he can't or won't. I say *he* because women are less likely than men to seek satisfactions which detach them from their community. Working-class women are usually too busy holding the community together.

So who will tell good stories about the people in Britain who still labour with their hands? Who can write a whole novel about (for example) an unambitious bricklayer? Someone whose culture and education have made him a manual worker, and who likes manual work, but finds there is less and less of it to be had? Someone who lives in a housing estate which was thought a great gift to the lowly paid in 1950 because each flat had an inside lavatory, but which otherwise has fewer amenities than an army barrack? I fear that no talented male author could embody himself in such a man for 127 pages without feeling stifled or wanting to rave or do something violently nasty. It is true that Mac, at the start of the "Up Country" chapter, flings a glass across a pub out of rage at the dull bigotry of the surrounding conversation, but despite his scars he is conventional in his judgements and kindly in his actions, though his judgements and actions tug in opposite directions. His feelings towards the hippy German tourist and poor Tolworth McGee are as dismissive as those of anyone else in his community, yet the hippy and McGee get all the companionship and assistance he can offer them. Like his companions in that part of the community which is no longer employable, he is a *gentle* man. I cannot imagine the social pressures which would drive him to riot. He is a socialist, living in a labour-voting area, but has no expectations that the Labour Party or trade union action will do anything to help him. If, to the three million unemployed Britons at the time of writing (October 1985) we add twice as many casual labourers whose work is part-time or threatened, then Mac is typical of a huge piece of Britain. Conservatives can draw soothing morals from his existence. I hope they will not.

Why read about this man? Is *Gentlemen* a dod of social reality we should dutifully rub our noses on because so many folk are sunk down in it? Yes, if you like reading for that reason, but I read it first because I found it funny. Indeed, I thought the first two chapters too funny by half, the characters a mere grotesque bunch of comic proles. Many popular tales about the poorer classes exploit that sort of condescension in the reader. Had the other chapters been equally facetious, *Gentlemen* would have been as enjoyable in small doses, and as disappointing on the whole, as any book by O. Henry or Damon Runyon. But I think Agnes Owens writes better than those good Americans. As her hero's stories accumulate they become a real novel, a moving picture of a hard, surprising world which is forcing a young man to understand both it and himself. The fun is not in the casual violence of oaths, black eyes and falling down drunk. The narrator takes these for granted but does not dwell on them, for he usually wants to avoid them. The fun is in the comedy of mainly decent people misunderstanding themselves and each other. This is the social essence of all comedy from *A Midsummer Night's Dream* to *What Ho, Jeeves!* The council flat, the Paxton Arms, the building site and the wino squat are not grotesque anarchies but societies maintained, like all societies, by affection and by codes. The affection is usually invisible, because the codes regard it as a dangerous weakness. The codes promote much misunderstanding because nobody knows all of them. The mother sells a box of tools her son has kept under her bed for years. She cannot grasp that, like crown jewels in the Tower of London, they are not for use but for status:

"Wait a minute," I said, scarcely able to credit my ears. "You didny gie him ma set o' tools that took me two years tae pay up when I was an apprentice brickie?"

"Well, ye never had them oot the box far as I can remember."

"Ye don't understand," I said slowly, my head beginning to ache. "Ye never use your own tools if ye can help it. Ye always nick someone else's. If ye took your own tools they wid just get nicked."

She was unperturbed. "How should I know that?"

By the last chapter our man has been unemployed

for several months, his only close friend has died of drink and exposure, and he has been arrested as accessory to an unusually futile crime. Heavy drinking has so washed out his chances of a sex-life that he has never considered one, and this is lucky. In his community sex leads to children and marriage, and who would gladly bring children into such a community? It is collapsing. The only choice is, collapse with it or clear out. If he had children his decent instincts would lead him to collapse with it. So his worst habit allows him a hopeful ending.

I began the last paragraph but two with an extended rhetorical question which I had better answer. *Gentlemen of the West* could only be written by someone who knew and liked building-workers and, without approving the harsh parts of their lives, found release, not confinement, in imagining them. It had to be written by a mother.

MORE ABOUT PENGUINS, PELICANS, PEREGRINES AND PUFFINS

For further information about books available from Penguins please write to Dept EP, Penguin Books Ltd, Harmondsworth, Middlesex UB7 0DA.

In the U.S.A.: For a complete list of books available from Penguins in the United States write to Dept DG, Penguin Books, 299 Murray Hill Parkway, East Rutherford, New Jersey 07073.

In Canada: For a complete list of books available from Penguins in Canada write to Penguin Books Canada Ltd, 2801 John Street, Markham, Ontario L3R 1B4.

In Australia: For a complete list of books available from Penguins in Australia write to the Marketing Department, Penguin Books Australia Ltd, P.O. Box 257, Ringwood, Victoria 3134.

In New Zealand: For a complete list of books available from Penguins in New Zealand write to the Marketing Department, Penguin Books (N.Z.) Ltd, Private Bag, Takapuna, Auckland 9.

In India: For a complete list of books available from Penguins in India write to Penguin Overseas Ltd, 706 Eros Apartments, 56 Nehru Place, New Delhi 110019.